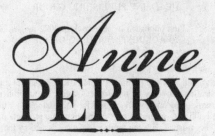

# Anne
# PERRY

# A
# CHRISTMAS
# LEGACY

HEADLINE

First published in 2021 by
HEADLINE PUBLISHING GROUP

First published in paperback in 2022 by
HEADLINE PUBLISHING GROUP

1

Cataloguing in Publication Data is available from the British Library

ISBN 978 1 4722 7514 1

Typeset in Times New Roman PS by Palimpsest Book
Production Limited, Falkirk, Stirlingshire

Printed and bound in Great Britain by Clays Ltd, Elcograf S.p.A.

HEADLINE PUBLISHING GROUP
An Hachette UK Company
Carmelite House
50 Victoria Embankment
London EC4Y 0DZ

www.headline.co.uk
www.hachette.co.uk

To all who are willing to fight for others

'How old are you?' Gracie asked sternly.

'I'm very almost six,' Charlie replied, taking her finger away from the mixing bowl in which the Christmas cake was being stirred for the final time, and looking at her mother with a combination of awe and pleading.

Gracie regarded her daughter with as much severity as she could manage, which was not a lot. 'So you know to wait until I'm finished and have put this into the cake tin, and then the oven. Then you can have it.'

'But you don't leave anything,' Charlie said reasonably.

'I leave enough,' her mother replied, and started to spoon the mixture into the baking tin. It was rich with raisins, sultanas, candied orange peel, and everything else delicious, even tiny threepenny bits, wrapped in pieces of cloth, so nobody would accidentally swallow them.

'How long is it till Christmas?' Charlie asked again.

'A week and two days,' Gracie replied.

'Why does everybody have a party for another little boy?' Charlie asked. 'We aren't going to have another little boy, are we? We've got enough.' She had two younger brothers, aged four and three. She was quite sure they did not need any more.

'This one was special,' Gracie explained.

'You said ours were special, too,' Charlie reminded her.

'Special to us. The one at Christmas is special to everybody.' Gracie moved the spoon round the bowl for a last time and regarded it carefully.

'That's enough!' Charlie said quickly. 'You can't take it all!'

Gracie handed her the bowl and the spoon. 'Can you manage that?'

'Course I can!' Charlie answered without hesitation. She took the spoon and began licking off the very last scraps of cake mixture.

Before she had finished, there was a knock on the kitchen door at the back of the house. It opened to the scullery, and outside to the yard where the rubbish bins and the coal scuttles were, and, of course, where deliveries were made.

Gracie went to answer it. Her daughter followed close behind.

On the step was a girl of perhaps fourteen. She was dressed in a warm coat and she was wearing a hat, but she looked miserable, even frightened.

'Mrs Tellman?' she asked. 'Gracie Tellman?' She was ready to run away, if Gracie denied it.

'Yes, that's me,' Gracie answered. 'Come in. You look half perished with cold.'

She stepped back and opened the door wider so the girl could come inside. Gracie could see that she was in service. Before she was married, Gracie had been in service herself. But unlike so many girls, she had the good fortune to be in service to only one family, the Pitts. She had been thirteen when she started, and well over twenty when she left to marry Samuel Tellman. He had been a junior policeman then. Now he was an inspector at the Bow Street station, one of the most famous in London.

The girl came in and stood shivering in the kitchen. She was not much more than five feet tall, standing eye-to-eye with Gracie.

Gracie pointed to one of the chairs at the kitchen table and she sat down. It was the chair nearest the stove. Without asking, Gracie filled the kettle and put it on the hob.

'I don't know if you remember me,' the girl began tentatively. 'My name is Millie Foster.'

Memory flooded back to Gracie's mind. A case Samuel had first told her about late one evening, sharing his day with her when the children had gone to bed. It was her favourite time. All the work was done, the doors were closed. Samuel would tell her not just about the job, but also the things that had moved him, funny or sad or difficult. In some cases, she had even become involved herself. Suddenly, at the mention of her name, Gracie remembered Jenny Foster and her daughter, Millie, who had been about Charlie's age then, and wrongly accused of household theft. Jenny had been charged with being unfit to look after her only child. It was Tellman, with a lot of help from Gracie, who had proved her innocence and reunited them. They had remained friends until Jenny's early death, five or six years after that.

'Yes, of course,' Gracie said warmly, and then without any warning her eyes filled with tears, the memory sharp and touched with guilt. There was

4

nothing she could have done to save Jenny. It was a sudden and devastating illness. But Millie had been taken in by an aunt, and Gracie had lost touch with her.

Now she looked at the distress in the girl's face and did not waste time in regretting the past. 'What's wrong?' she asked.

Millie shook her head. 'It's not theft like before. We don't know what it is. Leastways, *I* don't. And I don't think anybody else does.' She paused for a moment, as if not certain how to explain. 'A lot of food goes missing, the nicest things, like cakes and pudding and cream. And pieces of chicken, stuff like that … but no one says anything about it.'

'Oh.' Grace's mind raced. If the missing food was sufficient that a housemaid knew about it, then it was surely only a matter of time before the mistress of the house knew as well. Then somebody would be thrown out, without a reference, at best. At worst, they might even be charged with stealing. 'You really have no clue who's taking it?' she asked.

'No. And it doesn't go at night. It goes all times. Sometimes I think it's one person, but then it looks like it can't be.'

'Have you got mice? Or worse?'

'No, we ain't!' Millie said vehemently. 'If you've got mice you can see where they've been. They leave droppings and such. Besides, we got a cat, and she's a good mouser. One smell of a cat, and the mice go elsewhere. We covered it up, the missing stuff, much as we can, but everybody's scared.'

'Everybody?' Gracie asked with some doubt.

'Yeah,' Millie nodded vehemently. 'Even Mr Denning!'

'Who's he?'

'The butler. And he don't scare easy. Something real bad is happening. Somebody's got to know. But nobody's telling.' She put her arms across each other and hugged herself protectively.

'We'll find out,' Charlie offered. She knew for whom she said it. 'My mam's the best 'tective anywhere. She'll find out for you.'

Gracie interrupted quickly. 'No, I'm not! You mustn't say that.'

'Daddy says it,' Charlie defended herself instantly. And she wasn't making it up. She got into trouble if she said things that were not true.

'He was … exaggerating,' Gracie argued.

Charlie was puzzled. 'Was … what?'

Gracie did not know how to answer without

implying that her husband had said something that was not true, or that possibly he did not know what he was talking about.

Gracie abandoned the argument for a few moments while she made the tea and fetched a wedge of cake out of the pantry. She cut it into two large pieces and a small one for herself, put them on plates and passed one to Millie, who appeared to have relaxed a little as she was beginning to warm up, and the other to Charlie.

Charlie thanked her mother with a big smile. 'I like this,' she said to Millie. 'You'll like it, too.'

'You like everything,' Gracie said, then smiled apologetically at Millie.

'I don't like pa-turnips,' Charlie corrected her.

Millie looked puzzled. 'Pa-turnips?'

'You know,' Charlie explained. 'Potatoes and pa-turnips. Only potatoes are nice.'

'Oh, yes.' Millie understood now. 'I agree.' She smiled, but there were tears in her eyes.

'Don't worry,' Charlie assured her. 'Mam will fix it.'

Gracie looked at her daughter's smooth, innocent little face, and the certainty in it. She wasn't speaking for herself, but for the frightened girl who sat next to her, still wrapping her coat tightly around her as if it were some kind of armour. Against what? Fear? Rejection? Blame for the disappearing food?

'Mam?' Charlie prompted her. 'Daddy and I will look after everybody here ... and I'll help, I promise.'

Millie's face reflected real hope for the first time.

Gracie took a deep breath. 'If I go to your house for a few days, will you stay here and look after mine? Can you do the laundry? Even sheets? Anyone can sweep, but can you cook? And look after my little boys as well?'

Millie's face filled with light. 'I got five cousins I looked after, when me mam died and me aunt took me in. And Charlie here will show me where everything is ...' She stopped just short of adding *please*, but it was in her face.

'I'll be good,' Charlie promised. 'All the time,' she added.

'You are good,' Gracie said honestly. 'Nearly all the time.'

Charlie turned to Millie. 'See? Mam will make it all right.'

Millie shut her eyes and let out her breath, as if a great weight had been lifted from her shoulders.

Gracie was trapped, and she knew it. 'What am I supposed to say happened to you?' she asked Millie.

'She's sick,' Charlie answered before Millie could speak. 'You are just taking her place till she's better.' After a moment, her face became serious. 'You'll be home, won't you? Before it's Christmas?'

'Most certainly I will!' Gracie said, very firmly indeed.

'Promise?' Charlie insisted. She knew promises must never be broken, no matter what.

'Yes, darling, I promise. And you must promise to be patient with Tommy and Vic. They're only little, they don't understand as much as you do. You'll be standing in for me, so you must make sure Daddy tells them a story at bedtime. No excuses!'

Charlie nodded. 'Yes, I promise.'

'And while I look after Millie's house, you must help her look after ours. Can you do that?'

'Yes,' said Charlie, nodding solemnly.

'And don't be too bossy!' Gracie added, trying not to smile.

Charlie thought about that one for a moment or two. 'How can I promise everything will be looked after if I can't tell them what to do?'

Gracie wondered how a 'very almost six-year-old'

could, at times, be so horribly logical. 'How about not telling them, but asking them?' she suggested.

Charlie thought for a moment or two, as if wondering if she was obliged to agree.

Before she could speak, Gracie asked, 'Millie, how did you know to come here?'

Millie gave a shy smile. 'Me mam used to talk about you. I just knew that, with things so bad, I should ask you.' She lowered her eyes. 'If you can't help, I understand, it being nearly Christmas an' all, but I had to try.' After a pause, she added, 'With Mam ... dead ... I didn't know where else to go.'

Gracie could feel Charlie's eyes on her. It was as if she were thinking about everything Gracie had told her about helping people, good manners, patience, sharing. 'Yes,' she said to Millie. 'You stay here and look after my house, the best you can. And I'll see if I can find out what's wrong.'

Millie's face flooded with relief. 'I will, I promise,' she said eagerly.

Charlie greeted the answer with a shining smile.

'I'll show you where everything is,' Gracie said. 'And if you forget, Charlie will remind you.'

\*

'You what?' Tellman said when he came home, and Gracie told him what she planned to do. 'You can't!' He looked tired and cold, and extremely glad to be warm at last, and be able to take off his wet coat and boots. 'Gracie! It's almost Christmas.'

Gracie felt a sharp twinge of guilt. She knew that. A time for paying old debts, for not turning your back on anyone. A time for giving, not getting. 'Samuel,' she said gently, trying to keep the sharpness out of her voice. This must be handled very carefully, if she were to succeed; carefully, and without any anger. She could not leave the house with ill feeling between them, however temporary. Neither could she deny Millie with any easy conscience. Fairly or not, she would blame Samuel for it, even if she did not mean to. It was unfair. She had been at home all day while he had been out dealing with other people's violence and tragedies.

He was listening, waiting, but she knew that he would not remain like this much longer, in silence.

'Samuel,' she said quickly. 'There could be something really wrong in that house, I mean badly! We can't shut the door on them and not even look.' She lowered her voice. 'That's what Charlie will see. That we don't care, if it's uncomfortable for us. Our children copy us. You know that. Just watch Tommy: he walks the way you do; he says the same words you use, even when he doesn't know what they mean. He asks you for help, to show him how to do things, because he trusts you, and he knows you won't deny him. Refusing to help when someone asks – this isn't the lesson we want to teach them.'

'All right!' he said sharply, cutting off further argument he must know was coming. There was disappointment in his face, but acceptance, even understanding. 'But you'll be home for Christmas! That's not a suggestion, Gracie. I mean it.'

'Yes, Samuel. You have two weeks off now, so you'll be here, and Charlie will help you.'

'She's five years old,' he protested, the beginning of panic in his eyes. 'I can't make her work. I won't!'

Gracie struggled against the urge to smile. 'No,' she agreed. 'Not work, but you'll let her help. She'd be so proud of that, and she can tell you what I do and how I do it … most of the time. It might take longer, but let her help you. It would be the best Christmas present you could give her.' That was not an exaggeration. For Charlie, nothing was worth more than her father's approval.

Tellman gave her a half-smile and let out a loud

sigh. 'Fine, I'll look after them. But Gracie,' he added, resuming his head-of-the-household voice, 'we have a telephone. You send a message every day saying that you're all right. And if you don't, I'll be there to ask you why not. And I mean that, too.'

She did not need to press the issue. She could see in his face that he would be as good as his word. All the years she had known him – long before she'd even thought that he loved her, never mind when she realised that he did – he had always been very serious about his word. It was one of the earliest things she had liked about him. There was trust long before there was love. 'Yes, I will, every day,' she said.

Gracie knew too well why Millie was afraid. She had never worked in a bad house, but she certainly had heard about them. You dare not answer back, and you choose to say nothing because if you do, you can be put out, without a character reference, and you're on the street. That idea was so dreadful she didn't want to say it out loud. It was every servant's nightmare.

Tellman touched her cheek very gently. 'You can't solve the world's problems, Gracie. But I remember Jenny, too. And I suppose you can't turn your back on her now. Take a look and see if there really is something terrible going on in that house. But don't run any risks there. Your main job is here. We need you.'

She knew then that she had his approval. She didn't put it at risk by adding anything more. She merely gave him a radiant smile and thanked him.

'You have to get a reference to take with you,' he pointed out. 'A really good one that they can't ignore. It's no good me writing it. I'll go and ask Lady Pitt.' He smiled when she gasped. 'You worked for her since you were a child. When I tell her what this is for, she'll agree.'

Of course, she would! Charlotte Pitt had known Gracie since she was thirteen. She had taught Gracie to read and write. She had shared with Gracie her own part – one might have described it as meddling – in her husband's cases. Quite often, Gracie herself had actually helped. Thomas Pitt had been a young policeman then. Perhaps Lady Pitt was still meddling, even though her husband was head of Special Branch for all of England.

Gracie breathed out slowly. 'Thank you, Samuel. That would be … wonderful.'

\*

Tellman rode with Gracie in a hansom cab right up to the pavement outside the back door of the Harcourts' home, not more than two miles from their own, but in fashionable Eaton Square. Socially, it was a world away.

'I'm going to wait outside here for ten minutes,' he told her. 'And if you're not out by then, I'll take it that you're staying.' He leaned forward and kissed her gently. 'Don't forget to telephone! If you don't call, I'll be round here after you. You have the number. This is 1900, Gracie; I can get here in ten minutes, if I need to. You don't let anyone push you around.'

She smiled at him in the shadow of the cab. Although there were automobiles on the street now, there were still plenty of horse-drawn vehicles, too.

'I have to find out what's wrong here,' she told him. She kissed him again, quickly, then before he could close his arms around her, she bent and picked up the handle of her suitcase and walked to the servants' entrance, the back door of Harcourt House. She did not look back at him in case it weakened her resolve. She was already wondering if this was such a good idea. What could she do if there really was anything more than a bit of bullying going on?

It happened in lots of houses. If you called in the police, it would only make it worse. They would believe the master before any servant, and after they had gone, it would be redoubled.

She knocked on the scullery door, her heart thumping so hard that whoever answered must surely hear it. She was about to knock again when the door opened and a tall and very handsome young man stood there looking down at her.

'Yes?' he asked.

It was not too late to pretend she had come to the wrong door. But what would she say to Millie? Or to Charlie? Or, for that matter, to Charlotte Pitt, after whom Charlie was named?

She coughed and cleared her throat, but her voice was a kind of squeak. 'Hello, my name is Gracie Tellman, and I've come to tell you that Millie Foster is sick, but I'm here to take her place, just for a few days.'

The man was momentarily stuck for words.

She seized the chance. 'I have a reference, from Lady Pitt, the last place I worked.'

'Why did you leave?' he asked.

'Got married, didn't I? I'm just coming till Millie gets better.'

'So, what does your husband say about this then?' the young man asked sceptically.

'He brought me here. He reckons it's the right thing to do, so Millie doesn't lose her place.'

'You got that reference, Mrs …?'

'Tellman. Gracie Tellman. Yes, I have.' She brought it out of her coat pocket and handed it to him. She was annoyed that her hand was shaking. She hoped he would think it was the cold: the wind was like ice along the passage.

He took it from her, opened it and read it slowly. He probably did not have much occasion to read.

Gracie stood shivering on the step. It seemed like ages. She was aware of the hansom cab still at the kerb, with Samuel inside, watching her. The horse was shifting its weight from foot to foot. 'My husband's still waiting so he can see me safely inside. He's in that cab. His name is Inspector Tellman, from Bow Street.'

'That right?' The man's voice was laden with doubt. 'Then I'll go ask him.' He folded up the letter, but kept hold of it, then he walked around Gracie and down the short path towards the gate, then out into the street. He returned in what seemed like an age, but was probably no more than two or three minutes.

She tried to ask him what had happened, but her voice was only a clearing of the throat, no more.

'Come in, Mrs Tellman. I promised the inspector I'd look after you. But I think we best call you Gracie, like the others, if that's all right.'

'That's fine,' she replied, overwhelmed with relief.

He picked up her case and carried it inside for her. 'I'm Walters,' he said, 'valet to Mr Harcourt. And footman, when they need one.'

She followed him, closing the scullery door behind her. It felt frighteningly final, the end of one world and the beginning of another, where she was no longer mistress of her time, to do as she pleased.

Walters led her along the corridor to the house-keeper's sitting room and knocked on the door, then stood back waiting for an answer.

After a long moment, it was opened by a woman of medium height, but so thin it made her seem even taller. Her face was gaunt, but it spoke of both intense intelligence and a high sensitivity. She had a prominent aristocratic nose and large brown eyes. She was wearing a very plain woollen dress that seemed no colour at all, and there was a large bunch of keys hanging from her leather belt.

'What is it, Walters?' she asked. In the shadows

of the corridor, she did not immediately notice Gracie.

'Mrs Jenkins, this is Gracie Tellman. Apparently, our Millie is sick, and Gracie has come to take on her duties ... so Millie doesn't lose her position. She has excellent references, from Lady Pitt, wife of Sir Thomas Pitt, the head of Special Branch.' He said that as if he knew what it was.

Mrs Jenkins' rather sketchy eyebrows rose. 'And how will Lady Pitt do without Gracie?' she asked. Her voice was soft and very precise.

Gracie drew in her breath to answer, but the footman got there before her. 'She doesn't work there any more, Mrs Jenkins. She left to get married, to a senior policeman at Bow Street.'

'Is that what she told you?' Mrs Jenkins enquired, her wispy eyebrows raised again.

'No, Inspector Tellman told me that himself. He brought her and I checked with him. I saw his police identity card,' Walters replied.

Mrs Jenkins looked at Gracie. 'And why are you willing to do this, Mrs Tellman?' Her lips formed a thin line. 'What money do you expect?'

'For a few days?' Gracie asked. 'I don't expect any money. It's a Christmas present, if you like. Poor

Millie's got a terrible cold. A few days off will cure it.'

'Do you think so? You are a doctor as well?' Mrs Jenkins said sarcastically.

'I have three children. Colds come and go,' Gracie replied, and immediately knew that it was an error.

'I see. And who is going to look after these three children while you are here doing Millie's job?' Mrs Jenkins asked.

'My husband, o' course. He's got a couple of weeks' holiday. But I'll be home by Christmas, because Millie will be better.' Gracie said that with certainty, hoping it was true about her going home. It had to be. She had given Samuel and, more importantly, Charlie her word.

'Well, I suppose you'll be better than nothing,' Mrs Jenkins conceded. 'You can have Millie's room, for the time being. And you can start tomorrow morning. You're on trial, you understand?'

'Yes, Mrs Jenkins,' Gracie answered obediently.

'Go with Walters. He'll take you upstairs and introduce you to Nora, our parlour maid, with whom you will work. And, of course, the between-stairs maid, Bessie. Breakfast will be at seven o'clock tomorrow morning, in the servants' dining room.

Someone will waken you at half past six. You will meet the butler, Mr Denning, tomorrow. Welcome to Harcourt House.'

'Thank you, Mrs Jenkins,' Gracie said with relief. She was happy to follow Walters up the backstairs, reserved for the servants, leading up to the attic floor, where their bedrooms were, and the bathroom for the female staff. The bedrooms and bathroom for the male staff – the butler, the footman and the boot boy – would be in a separate wing of the house.

Gracie thanked Walters. When he had gone and the door was closed, she stared around the room. She had never had a room like this, right under the roof, with one small dormer window in the sloping ceiling, and no fireplace. Thank heaven there was a thick eiderdown on the bed. There was one chest of drawers with a looking-glass above it, and a chair and bedside table and lamp. There was one picture hanging on the wall that backed on to the passage. It was a country scene with trees and a small cottage. A reminder of Millie's home? Or an idealised picture, painted from the artist's memory and imagination? Either way, it was a comfortable image, an escape from the present, from work and thoughts of being a stranger in somebody else's home. A home in which making one mistake could have you turned out on to the street.

That thought hardened Gracie's resolve to stay here. She admitted ruefully that she had been in Harcourt House for only half an hour, and she was already doubting her decision to come. Was Millie's fear real? Wasn't she just a young girl, out of her depth so far from home, having to work and live with people she hardly knew?

Gracie unpacked her case and put her clothes away, hung up her plain dark dress in the wardrobe and put out her regular, comfortable boots, ready for tomorrow. She made a quick visit to the bathroom, then came back to bed. It took her a long time to fall asleep. She was troubled, lonely, and cold as well. And she was not at all sure if she was going to accomplish anything. Was it possible that she might even make whatever the matter was worse?

She woke sharply to see the room still dark, except for the crack of light from the passage. A little girl with dark, curly hair was peeping around the door. She looked to be about twelve. Gracie blinked and for a moment wondered where on earth she was. Then she remembered. This was Harcourt House.

She had come here last night. Only for a few days. 'Hello,' she said. 'Who are you?'

'Bessie.' The girl gave a tentative smile. 'I'm the tweeny. It's time to get up. What's your name?'

'Hello, Bessie. My name is Gracie. How old are you?'

'Thirteen.' That was said with pride. Gracie guessed it was a very recent birthday.

Gracie smiled. 'I'll be down in the kitchen in ten minutes. I'm hungry.'

Bessie gave a wide smile, then slipped out of the door, closing it behind her.

Gracie was as good as her word, and ten minutes later she was washed, dressed, and had found her way down the backstairs to the servants' dining room. It was a bit cramped, with a large table in the centre, surrounded by ten mismatched, hard-backed wooden chairs. Seven of them were occupied. She recognised the housekeeper, Mrs Jenkins, sipping a cup of tea. There was nothing on her plate but a slice of toast. But Gracie was looking for the butler who, in all practical ways, was the head of the household.

She had already met Walters, the footman, and the red-haired boot boy was obvious. He was about the same age as Bessie, twelve or thirteen, far nearer

Charlie's age than Gracie's. Of course, she knew why children were employed here. She had first gone to the Pitts' house when she was thirteen because there was not enough room for her, or food to go around, in her own ever-growing family.

The butler was looking at her. He had fair, curling hair, thinning a little now, and a pleasant face, weathered, and there was a faint scar on his left cheek. 'Morning, sir,' she said, careful to show respect.

'Good morning, Gracie,' he replied, looking grateful that she had instantaneously seen him as the head of the house. 'Sit down and have breakfast.'

She sat obediently and she was served with toast and a hard-boiled egg, and more toast with marmalade. And, of course, a cup of tea.

He introduced the other servants: the pleasant-faced cook with her hair straying from her cap, which was intended to keep it out of the way. The lady's maid, thin and dark haired, dark eyed, with delicate black brows. Hers was a fierce face, but relaxed, smiling – if she ever did – she might have been beautiful, in her own way. The kitchen maid, with softly curling red-brown hair and freckles, like the red-haired boot boy. The handsome, fair-haired parlour maid with a peaches-and-cream complexion.

Gracie said hello to all of them and received smiles and nods in return.

She sat almost silently eating breakfast, watching as much as would seem natural for a stranger trying to settle in, all the time wondering what she could do to learn what it was that had frightened Millie so badly. Or was the girl actually imagining it all?

The morning passed quickly, because there was so much to do. The first duty was to clear out all the grates and light the fires throughout the house, beginning with those in the rooms used most often. She started in the withdrawing room, where Mrs Harcourt would wish to entertain callers, should they come, so the room must be dusted, tidied and the floor swept, including the carpets. Before that, the grate must be cleared out, the new fires laid, and the coal buckets filled. The master's study was next, although it was unlikely anyone would want to sit there, even Mr Harcourt himself. It was not the housemaid's job to see to the kitchen oven fires, or keep the kitchen and the scullery clean. The kitchen maid, Mary, would do that.

Bessie, the dark little tweeny, would clean the stairs and landings, and help Gracie with the bedrooms. The beds must be aired, then remade, and everything left dusted, tidied and neat. Any laundry must be removed and taken downstairs to the laundry room. Miss Allsop, the lady's maid, would see to Mrs Harcourt's clothes and linen. Walters, the valet, would be sure Mr Harcourt's suits were clean and pressed, his boots polished, and anything else his master might wish.

Why was she here at all? It was so different from working at home. It was not that there was more to do in this house: there wasn't. It was the feeling that the work was pointless. The house was very little lived in. There were no children, no pet animals, other than the cat, which she had not yet seen and which apparently was restricted to the kitchen area. Gracie missed the cat that she had at home, a patient creature that hardly ever scratched or bit, in spite of being grasped by children and solemnly lectured to. All the children's lessons on history and geography were repeated to the cat, who appeared to be listening. Charlie did not like dolls, so the cat was spared being dressed up, but it was directed to pay attention, which it seemed to enjoy.

Before lunch, there was a delivery of flowers to the back door. Mary took them in, and half an hour later Gracie accidentally found Mrs Jenkins, the housekeeper, in the scullery carefully sorting them and cutting away some of the extra leaves. Her thin face was intent on what she was doing, but she was smiling, almost as if the flowers were hers. She had two vases ready, one with filigree around the top, the other of plain apricot-coloured porcelain. She put one long-stemmed red rose into the coloured vase, then a russet-coloured chrysanthemum, and another. She stepped back to look at the effect, and suddenly became aware of Gracie. She swung round sharply, as though she had been caught doing something embarrassing, such as trying on the mistress's clothing.

Gracie had the feeling that Mrs Jenkins had been dreaming for a few minutes, imagining these flowers were hers, and the sudden wave of colour in the woman's face betrayed her. Gracie had sprigs with holly berries on her own kitchen windowsill, and remembered the pleasure of arranging the twigs. 'You make that look special,' she said to the housekeeper.

'Thank you,' Mrs Jenkins answered quietly 'They need to be seen. Each one, not just as a whole.' She stopped, as if perhaps not wishing to say the rest of her thought aloud.

'Like people,' Gracie said for her.

Mrs Jenkins turned away. 'Yes.' She cut off another stalk. 'The kitchen's to the left, if you're lost.'

'Thank you,' Gracie replied. She had turned the wrong way. She went out and along the corridor into the kitchen.

The cook's name was Mrs Bland, but everyone called her simply Cook. She looked up and her face lit when she saw Gracie. Automatically, she tucked a strand of hair back under her cap.

'Ah! How's your first day? You don't know where everything is, but you'll soon learn.' She had been rolling pastry, but she stopped for a few moments, leaning on the table with the rolling pin covered with flour still in her hands. 'You plan on staying long? What I mean is, is Millie going to be all right?' Her pleasant face was creased with anxiety.

Gracie was undecided what to say, exactly. Millie wasn't ill, but she was scared. And Cook was concerned for her.

'Yes,' she said. 'She just needs a day or two's rest. By the time she's looked after my three children, she could be glad to be back here.' She saw even before she was finished that Cook did not believe her.

Should she tell Cook the truth? It was sooner than she had meant to. She could get thrown out, and then what would she have accomplished? She would have made it worse. And where would Millie go then? She would not only be without a job, she would be without a home, in the middle of winter. And she would never find another place without a good character reference. Maybe it was too late already. And if Gracie did discover the truth, would Millie come back here? Was there anything here really different from any other house? Maybe she wasn't ready to go into service yet. But what else was there? Working in a factory, like part of an engine, nothing personal, nothing individual at all? And where would she live?

Cook must have been watching Gracie's face, because she interrupted her thoughts.

'Is she sick, Gracie? She's one of us. We care about her.'

'She's not really badly sick,' Gracie replied. 'Just got a cold, and tired and, at the bottom of it all, scared.'

Cook frowned, a shadow over her face. 'Did she say what about? What she's scared of?'

'No, she didn't say. Not really.' Gracie had already painted herself into a corner.

Cook stood without moving for several seconds, then she sighed. 'We don't none of us know exactly what to be scared of. I suppose it's guilt.' She looked confused and miserable as she said it.

Gracie was confused, too. 'Guilt? For what?'

Something inside Cook's eyes closed off, as if the thought was suddenly lost. 'I don't know,' she said. 'Maybe I'm wrong.' She looked down at the pastry and put both her hands back on the rolling pin. 'I shouldn't judge. I don't know what she was frightened of.'

'Do you think she did something wrong?' Gracie hated asking, but she could see that Cook was avoiding the truth.

Cook stiffened. 'Certainly not! We none of us did anything wrong. We didn't!' She took a deep breath. 'Like nobody done anything wrong. It's her imagination. Millie needs to be able to talk about it, and then put whatever it is out of her mind.'

Gracie looked at Cook's troubled face and knew that there was nothing to be accomplished in arguing with her now. 'I'm sure you're right,' she agreed. 'Things get out of proportion sometimes.'

'Yes,' Cook agreed. 'You like stew? We've got a good stew for dinner tonight. Lamb and leeks, onions and white turnips. A little rosemary to sharpen it a bit.'

'Oh!' Gracie found a sudden lump in her throat at the thought of Charlie and her pa-turnips. 'I'd like to try that, it sounds wonderful. If I really like it, would you tell me how to make it? So, when I go back home …'

That was a surprise answer that Cook must not have foreseen, because a look of pleasure crossed her face. 'How many do you cook for?' she asked.

'Me and my husband, and three kids. They're nearly six, and four and three.'

'That's lovely,' Cook said with a smile that reflected both pleasure and a sudden awareness of something she had missed, both its burdens and its joys. She shook her head sharply, perhaps to bring herself back to reality. 'If you like it, I'll tell you what's in it. But I expect as you'll know.'

'Thank you,' Gracie said warmly.

That was enough for the moment. She must get back to work, or she would earn a reputation for talking too much and holding up other people from their chores.

After four that afternoon, tea was to be served in the withdrawing room for Mrs Harcourt and her two visitors. They were expected and Nora, looking her smartest with her uniform of a black dress and a white, lace-trimmed apron and cap, went to answer the doorbell. Parlour maids were chosen for their looks as much as their abilities. If they were tall and slender, and walked gracefully, it added a certain polish to the reputation of their mistress, and to the house in general. Similarly, footmen should be tall and, when in livery, have firm and shapely legs. At least, that used to be important when Gracie first went into service nearly twenty years ago.

Watching Nora walk, head upright, back straight, Gracie wondered how the shorter and dumpier Mrs Harcourt compared with her. Probably not so well!

Gracie was glad of a chance to sit down to a cup of tea after the guests in the drawing room were served and had settled into a lively exchange of plans and gossip. It was not a life Gracie wished for.

Nor had Charlotte Pitt wished for it! Although she came from a society background, she had married far beneath her, at that time, to a policeman, of all things. Certainly, it was many years ago now, when Thomas Pitt had been lower in rank than Samuel Tellman was currently. But Charlotte had become involved in many of his cases, especially where they concerned the higher levels of society. Which had been surprisingly often. Gracie had lived in, of course, and she had overheard a great deal about some of those people and events. The kitchen table had been the heart of the house. Gracie was the only resident servant, and she had been treated more like a friend, even a member of the family. She, too, had been drawn into thought and consideration of some of the murders that had shocked London. Those had been good days. But the fact that she really did love Samuel, and then the happiness and the hard work of children, all of this more than made up for not being involved in cases any more.

But she was sharply aware that her life with the Pitts had never been anything like the lives of the people who surrounded her now. There had been times of friendship, of course, and terror and danger as well. Defeat was always possible. And not every case was solved successfully. Many involved real tragedy. She recalled one event in particular when she had been out alone, after dark, during a series of hideous murders, in the East End of London. She had come upon one of the corpses, terribly mutilated. The horror of it still came back to her at times, perhaps once or twice every few years.

But there had never been the tension inside the house that she could feel here, sitting around the servants' dining table, trying to think of something harmless to say and watching the tense faces of the others.

It was half an hour later that she was unwittingly witness to a scene that distressed her. She was on her way upstairs to her bedroom, but using the main staircase because she had some clean linen to drop off in Mrs Harcourt's dressing room. She saw the between-stairs maid, Bessie, carrying a plate covered with a napkin, crossing the landing ahead of her.

Mrs Harcourt appeared, seemingly out of nowhere, but she must have been in Mr Harcourt's dressing room, because it was the only door out of sight of the stairs.

Bessie froze.

'And where are you going with that, Bessie?' Mrs Harcourt said in an ice-cold voice. Her eyes were wide, her black, finely plucked eyebrows arched.

Bessie gulped. Clearly, she had no answer. She must have believed the way was clear. She would have been out in the open, between the stairs and the door to the servants' quarters on this floor, for less than a minute.

'Well?' Mrs Harcourt demanded.

Gracie wished she knew what was on the plate

under the napkin, so she could say something, but she had no idea.

Neither of them seemed aware of Gracie standing near the wall on the top step of the long staircase.

Mrs Harcourt leaned forward and took the corner of the napkin between her thumb and forefinger, and then whipped the napkin away, revealing a large slice of sponge cake with raspberry jam and whipped cream. A clean spoon was balanced on one side of the plate.

'You greedy little thief!' Mrs Harcourt said between clenched teeth. 'Caught you at last! I suspected someone was stealing from the pantry, but I didn't know which one of you it was. But you all knew about it! Well, I've caught you now red-handed.'

Bessie's face burned, but she said nothing. Her eyes brimmed with tears.

'It's no good crying!' Mrs Harcourt said sharply. 'Tears mean nothing.'

Gracie's mind raced for something to do. What could she say that Mrs Harcourt would believe? She couldn't possibly let this child take the blame, even if she had taken food from the pantry. And, by the look of it, not the servants' pantry. None of their puddings or desserts had that much whipped cream on them. Nor did they eat with the best solid silver, like the monogrammed spoon on the edge of the plate. But what on earth could she say that would help?

'If I catch you once more, girl,' Mrs Harcourt went on, 'you'll be out in the street without a character. You're a thief, and I shall say so! You want to walk the streets looking for trade? What man would buy you for an hour? You skinny little ...' She gave up looking for a word that suited her mood, took the dish from the girl and turned on her heel. She went down the stairs and past Gracie who, apparently, she still had not noticed.

Instead of continuing to the landing, Gracie rushed towards the child standing alone.

Bessie lifted up her apron and used it to try to drown her sobs.

Gracie was shaking with rage, and furious also with herself that she had not been able to think of anything to defend the girl. She reached Bessie. Without giving it a thought, she put both arms around her and held her closely. She was barely two inches taller than Bessie, but she was almost old enough to be her mother. And she felt like it right now: a useless mother who had not been able to defend her child.

'Come on,' she said, stroking Bessie's hair. 'Stop crying and come downstairs. We best go down the backstairs. I'll find you something else to eat if you're still hungry. A piece of fresh bread and jam?'

Bessie sniffed hard and avoided Gracie's eyes. 'Weren't for me,' she said through her tears. 'And I daresn't get another piece.'

'Is that the truth, Bessie? And if it was for you, I don't blame you for wanting it. Just don't take it up the front stairs. That was foolish.'

'I was going to put this in Mrs Harcourt's dressing room.' She held out a rather crumpled silk petticoat.

'With a pudding in the other hand?' Gracie asked with doubt clear in her voice.

Bessie swallowed. 'Then go up with the pudding.'

'Up where? To your bedroom?'

Bessie shook her head, looking even more frightened than before.

'Well, I think we'd better go and iron that again. And Mrs Harcourt will just have to wait for it,' Gracie replied. 'And in the future, you better stay off the front stairs. Especially if you've got pudding in your hands!'

'But she's in this part of the house!' Bessie protested.

'Who is?' Gracie asked.

Bessie seemed too terrified to speak.

'Do you want to come down and get a slice of bread and jam?' Gracie suggested again. 'I'm sure Cook will let you have it. And maybe we could find a spoonful of cream to put on it.'

'It wasn't for me, miss,' Bessie said again.

'Who was it for?' Gracie asked. If this was a lie, it was a foolish one. Suddenly, she very fiercely did not want it to be. What sort of a future would this child have if she kept on telling lies? 'The truth, Bessie!'

'It were for her. She never gets nothing nice, less'en one of us takes it to her.'

'Who is "her"?'

Bessie's eyes widened with fear. 'I can't tell you. I don't … please, miss, don't tell no one I said anything … please?'

Gracie had no acceptable choice but to promise, although she was thoroughly confused. 'Now come to the backstairs with me and we'll go to the kitchen. I don't know about you, but I'd like another piece of bread and jam. That jam is terribly good. Does Cook make it herself?'

'Yes, miss.' Bessie nodded and sniffed away the

last of her tears. 'She's good to me and Archie. She don't tell us that we eat too much.'

Gracie felt a warmth for the cook float through her, an intense relief. 'Good,' she said. 'I've got three children, and they eat anything that isn't nailed down!'

''Ave yer?' asked Bessie, amazed. 'Then why do you live 'ere? Like a—' She stopped, aware that she had trespassed by asking questions that might be intrusive of another servant's very precious privacy. 'One of us?'

'It's just for a little while. To give Millie a few days to get well again,' Gracie answered. 'So ... I don't care what Mrs Harcourt thinks of me.'

Bessie was clearly fighting with herself whether to ask the next question or not.

Gracie realised what it was, and why it was so sensitive. 'My kids are all right. My husband's got time off because it's Christmas. He'll be there.'

Bessie smiled, and it filled her face with an image of something beautiful.

It was hard for Gracie to find an opportunity to use the telephone to call Samuel. But she had promised, and she knew he would keep his word to come here and fetch her if she did not call. For an instant, she wished she had not made such a rash commitment; then she was glad that she had. It was comforting to know that if she missed calling him, he would come looking for her. It was like having an extra blanket to tuck her in.

The telephone was in the hallway, a rather public place. She should not use it without asking. To do so risked major trouble, if she were caught. Who should she ask? Mr Denning? The butler was the most senior servant. But would he let her?

What about Walters? He knew that Samuel was a senior policeman, knew it himself, not just because she had said so. She winced as she thought what Samuel would say if he knew she had to ask permission to call him. He used to think it was wrong for anyone to be a servant, dependent on someone else's favour for their food and bed, living a life entirely directed by orders.

But that was when she had worked for the Pitts, ate good food at every meal, had a nice bedroom, and no fear of being dismissed. She thought it was far better than working in a factory, often being hungry and, more often still, cold. And able to be put out of work if she answered back. You were bound by circumstances, wherever you were! She and Samuel had had lots of arguments about this sort of thing. She smiled as she looked back on them now. They still argued, but there were no differences between them that mattered.

Walters. She would ask Walters.

She found him in the laundry room. He looked up from the table where he had been ironing Mr Harcourt's shirt.

'Mr Walters?' Gracie asked.

'What is it?'

She took a deep breath. 'I promised my husband I would telephone him every night, to tell him I'm all right. Please, may I use the telephone in the hall? I'll be very quick.'

He thought for a moment. 'And if you don't, then he'll come round here to find out why?' He smiled at the idea. 'Yes, you'd better do that. I'll come with you and make sure you don't have any difficulty.' He left the shirt where it was and went with her back to the main part of the house and into the hall, still smiling. The idea that a senior policeman might call at the house to make sure a servant was all right seemed to please him. She had hoped it would at least impress him.

They reached the telephone. Walters looked around, but no one was in sight. Mr and Mrs Harcourt were apparently in the withdrawing room with the door closed.

'There you are.' He indicated the instrument.

'Thank you.' Gracie picked up the mouthpiece and asked the operator for her own number. After only two rings, Samuel picked up at the other end.

'It's me,' Gracie said. She had used a telephone before, but she was not by any stretch of the imagination accustomed to it. The one at home was because of Samuel's work. 'I'm fine. How are the children? Is Charlie helping you?'

'She's helping a lot,' he said warmly, and Gracie guessed Charlie was standing right next to him listening. 'We are all well,' he went on. 'Can you tell me anything?'

'Not really. But I do need to be here.' She hoped he understood.

'Be careful, Gracie!' There was an unmistakable note of warning in his voice.

'I am, I promise. Say good night to them all for me.' She found her voice suddenly cracking. She longed so much for the feeling of the children's warm, wriggling little bodies in her arms. Vic particularly, because he wouldn't allow her to hold him, unless he was asleep.

'I will,' Samuel promised. 'Be careful.'

'Good night,' Gracie said and put the receiver down before she gave a hard sniff.

As if perhaps the woman had heard voices, Mrs Harcourt came to the withdrawing-room door, opened it and peered out into the hall.

Walters took Gracie's arm and pushed her towards the stairs. 'I'll show you,' he said to her, just loudly enough for Mrs Harcourt to hear and think Walters was helping Gracie find her way.

'Thank you.'

Mrs Harcourt went back into the withdrawing room.

'Thank you,' Gracie repeated, this time for Walters' benefit.

'Be careful,' he replied softly.

Tired as she was, Gracie found it difficult to sleep that night. She did not know what it was that Millie was afraid of, and yet she was acutely conscious of the prickle in the air that Millie had tried to describe. The scene on the landing had certainly been extraordinary.

She could not imagine Charlotte Pitt ever treating a servant, especially such a young one, as Mrs Harcourt had treated Bessie. When Gracie had been new to the Pitt house, she was the only servant – in fact, she was always the only servant to live in during all her years there – and she had sat with the family at each meal. It was not only common sense not to cook separately for one servant, it was also an ordinary decency that they never had to think about. But then, there were four of them, once the children came along, and only one of Gracie. In this house, there were only two family members, the two daughters, having grown up, were married and now living overseas. America, Cook had said. And there were ten servants. Feeding them like princes would be out of the question. Why did the Harcourts keep so many?

Gracie had to work hard at home now, with three children of her own. But she had help from Mrs Dunn, who came once a week to do the heavy laundry and give the floors and the outside steps a good hard scrub. It relieved Gracie, and gave Mrs Dunn a little extra money she could well use. Gracie had never found it difficult to let her do the work, or to pay her.

What did Mrs Harcourt do with her time? Was there anything that really pleased her? That gave her a sense of satisfaction, interest or achievement? Surely a happy woman would have told Bessie not to do it again, and then checked with Cook that the child was getting enough to eat.

What on earth was Bessie talking about when she mentioned 'going up with the pudding'? Should Gracie ask somebody, for example, Cook, who seemed to be the most approachable? Bessie clearly was too afraid to say. Was that because it was a lie? What did anybody know about Bessie? What was her home like? Did she miss it terribly or was it a joyful escape to be here? Did she ever get letters from her family? Stupid thought: she almost certainly could not read or write. Gracie herself had not been able to at thirteen. It was quite a few years before she finally allowed Charlotte to teach her. She could not imagine Mrs Harcourt putting in her time to teach the between-stairs maid to read and write!

Gracie finally fell asleep, attempting to think of a way to teach Bessie to read, and how that might be accomplished.

She woke in the morning with a start to see Mary, the kitchen maid, come to awaken her, carrying a mug of hot tea in her hand. It was a rude shock to her body when she got out of bed and realised how cold the room was. But then with no fire, and only days short of Christmas, what did she expect? She thanked Mary, sipped at the tea for a few moments, then washed and dressed hastily. She could not afford to miss breakfast.

The servants' dining room was exactly the same as it had been the previous day. Everyone sat in the same places, and Gracie took what was normally Millie's seat. The food was hot and fresh. Goodness knew what time Cook got up, in order to have the porridge smooth, creamy and cooked all the way through, and without a single lump. Young Archie, the boot boy, ate two complete bowls. Bessie, who was roughly the same age, accounted for a bowl and a half. Then there was any amount of fresh brown bread, a little butter, and Cook's own sharp, tangy, bitter orange marmalade, the kind Gracie had learned to make herself.

The morning passed busily with the usual cleaning tasks. Gracie even taught Bessie one or two tricks about polishing that the girl did not know. It was fun teaching her some of the things Gracie had learned over time, both as a maid and as a woman in her own house. There was not much ironing for a between-stairs maid to do, but Bessie very quickly understood how to time it so that one iron was heated while the other was in use. You had to test it always, with a few drops of water and a spare rag, to be sure it didn't burn the white linens. The delicate silks of Mrs Harcourt's blouses and dresses were Miss Allsop's task, and Mr Harcourt's shirts were the responsibility of Walters. It was a mistake to trespass on someone else's job unless requested to. To do so was forgivable … but only once.

The first break in the efficient running of the day came when Gracie saw Walters carrying a couple of hangers with clean shirts on them. One of the shirts slipped off the smooth wood and trailed a sleeve on the floor.

Young Archie went to pick it up and banged his head on Walters' chin as he, too, was leaning down, causing both clean shirts to fall.

Walters snapped at the boy.

'That's not fair!' Archie complained immediately, stung that his effort to help was so misunderstood. 'I was only—'

'Leave them alone,' Walters said, looking in disgust at the crumpled sleeve.

Gracie could see that Archie did not know what to do. He had no idea how to iron anything, or to get the grey smudge of dust off the shirt. To make it worse, Nora came into the passageway and saw immediately what had happened. She did not know how to help either, and while her natural sympathies were with Archie, she found Walters a great deal more attractive than she could afford to. Gracie had seen the glances between them and understood a lot of what could not be said.

Gracie was about to speak, although she could not think of anything really helpful to say, when Walters met Nora's eye for a moment and then flushed very slightly.

'Sorry, Archie,' he said. 'Not your fault, I know. I'll go and iron it again. I think the mark will come off without washing.'

'You can iron?' Archie said in amazement, confirming what Gracie has suspected: that he was new to the household. 'I thought women ...'

'Of course I can,' Walters replied. 'A good valet can do anything with the gentleman's clothes. If he's clever enough, he can even dress him to disguise that he's fat, or got knock knees.'

Nora stifled a laugh.

Archie's eyes were wide. ''As Mr Harcourt got knock knees, then?'

'And,' Walters went on, 'he never tells his master's secrets. Which he always knows.'

Archie's imagination raced; Gracie could see it behind his wide eyes.

Nora gave Walters a smile, which made him flush with pleasure, and he picked up the shirts. 'Come on,' he said to Archie, and without glancing back he went along the corridor with Archie behind him, trying to match his step, and having to put in a skip to keep up.

Gracie had seen Tommy do that with Samuel and it brought a ridiculous lump to her throat. She pretended not to notice, and returned to her original journey to the kitchen.

She spent the early part of the afternoon with the housekeeper, Mrs Jenkins. They were in the laundry, a large room separated from the kitchen and scullery, so that the people working in either did not distract each other, or stop to gossip. They were sorting the household linen, seeing what needed mending, or even replacing. It was the first time Mrs Jenkins had spoken to Gracie alone.

'I think this one's too thin to save.' She held up a

well-worn pillow slip. There was already one patch on it.

Gracie was surprised that a house like this, which kept so many servants, was willing not only to mend, but to patch domestic linens this way. 'Patching will just pull it further apart.'

'You're right,' Mrs Jenkins agreed. 'It won't last a week more.' She turned to one side and put the slip on a small pile of linens worn beyond use.

Her thinness, Gracie noticed, was not as if she had been left hungry, but as if it were her nature to be constantly worrying. The lines of anxiety on her thin face were deep enough to be visible, even when she relaxed. Her movements were quick and certain. She reached for the next sheet. It had already been turned sides to middle once. Gracie was familiar with the practice. When a sheet was well worn, you cut it right down the middle, hemmed the new edges, and joined the old ones to form a new centre. It was much less comfortable, but it would last another year or two, at least. She could remember her mother doing that, years ago, before she had left home. It was better than sleeping straight on the mattress ticking, which was scratchy on the skin.

She looked at the sheet and then up at Mrs Jenkins.

Mrs Jenkins opened her mouth, but instead of speaking, she just closed it with a sharp breath, and put the sheet on the pile to throw away. Was that tact … or fear?

They worked in silence. Gracie found a towel that Mrs Jenkins shook her head at, and added it to the pile of discards without comment.

They were interrupted by Nora, who looked at the pile on the floor with apparent surprise. 'All that to throw away, Mrs Jenkins? Are we getting new, then?'

'We're throwing away the old,' Mrs Jenkins snapped. 'It's just cluttering up the cupboards. We don't need linen with holes in it!'

'We've got a few dish towels as we could throw away then, and perhaps a petticoat or two,' Nora replied.

'You mind your tongue, miss! It might be your job to take good care of a few things, like buttons you wouldn't throw out, but it's not yours to criticise the household linen. What do you want in here anyway?' Mrs Jenkins looked at her sharply.

'I came for a clean tablecloth,' Nora replied quietly.

'You had one yesterday. You've spilled something on it already? We don't have a laundress here, and that tweeny maid can't iron a napkin, never mind a whole cloth. Scorch that once and it's ruined.' There was a look of disgust on Mrs Jenkins' face. Gracie could imagine expensive disasters of the past.

'I'm sorry, Mrs Jenkins.'

'So, you didn't spill something on it?' Mrs Jenkins asked.

Nora's head came up sharply. She was about to speak, then changed her mind. She held her hand out for the clean cloth.

Mrs Jenkins took several seconds, needing time to find the cloth Nora had requested. Finally, she produced it, looked at it for a moment, then gave it to her.

'Thank you, ma'am,' Nora said, and turned on her heel and left.

'Well!' Mrs Jenkins said under her breath.

'Who do you suppose really spilled something on that cloth?' Gracie asked.

Mrs Jenkins flushed painfully. She turned back to the pile of linens she had been looking through. 'I will not tolerate being lied to,' she said angrily, as if the rest were already explained.

Gracie knew that she should not say anything, but the words forced themselves out of her mouth. 'It's natural to protect one of the young ones. They'd be terrified of you telling Mrs Harcourt and their being out on the street in the cold, at Christmas.'

'Really, you are completely out of order!' Mrs Jenkins said, but she fumbled over the words, and her face was burning red. 'You are here under tolerance. I suggest you remember that. This time I will not report your impertinence to Mrs Harcourt, but watch your tongue, miss, or you are the one who will be …' Her voice trailed off.

'Out in the street?' Gracie finished for her. 'I won't. I'll go back to my husband and children, so you shouldn't try threatening me with that!'

Mrs Jenkins looked as if she'd been struck. She started to speak and stopped.

'I'm sorry,' Gracie said quietly. 'I'm lucky. I've got my own house, and my husband has a good job, and he's … he's clever at it. But I started out in service, the same age as the girls here. Sometimes I felt lonely, but not often.' She smiled at the memories crowding her mind. 'I had adventures, I did things that mattered, and I was treated like I belonged.' She was angry, and ashamed at some of the things she had just said, but she was also proud of the time she had been at the Pitts' house in Keppel Street.

Mrs Jenkins spoke so quietly Gracie could only

just hear her. 'I was too hard on Nora. We are all of us afraid right now. But I should be above that. I'm responsible for these girls. You included, while you're here. I'll go and find Nora.' She did not say to apologise to her, but it was implicit. She turned round and walked smartly out of the laundry room, her back stiff as a poker.

Gracie looked at the piles of sheets, pillowcases, towels and other linens, and continued to sort them. Now she knew exactly what Millie was trying to explain.

Even so, she was quite unprepared for what happened in the early evening. It was the last job she was going to do before staff supper. This meal was not something she was looking forward to, but she could not afford to miss it. She really was hungry and the food was one of those things in this unhappy house that was truly good. Cook could make almost anything taste special.

There was just this one task left to do, a very small thing: take the last bit of laundry up to the mistress's dressing room and hang it carefully.

She picked up the gown, and it was worthy of the name. It was no ordinary dress. On Mrs Harcourt, who was not very tall, it would be just above floor length. With high heels it would be perfect. And, of course, it was silk, the colour a pink so delicate, so luminous, it would make any wearer glow, feel beautiful, and, for moments at least, be certain everybody was looking at her admiringly.

Gracie had to hold it high so it did not trail and become soiled at the hem. Or worse than that, tripped over and torn. Her arms were aching by the time she crossed the landing to Mrs Harcourt's bedroom, and then through it to the adjoining dressing room, closing the door. There were several rails on which to hang clothes. Nevertheless, she had to make space by moving things around a little. Finally, there was a place for it and, on tiptoe, she hung it on the rail. It looked perfect.

She put her hand on the doorknob to open it and go back into the bedroom. She pulled it open silently.

Mrs Harcourt was standing in the centre of the bedroom floor. She had not heard anyone come in. She was facing Mr Harcourt.

The man was standing about five feet away from his wife, his body rigid, his face flushed. 'You've got to make a choice, Julia,' he said between his teeth.

'Like who, for heaven's sake?' she demanded. 'A thirteen-year-old maid without training? Gilbert, she can't even read! We pay her pennies, provide her food and a bed. We have the bed already, and her food is no more than we would waste every day.'

'I suppose you would tell me the other children are the same?' he said sarcastically. 'Young Archie has no appreciable use, and he eats like a horse!'

'Bread, Gilbert! Most of it is bread and potatoes,' she said with exaggerated patience.

'Then how about Allsop? We certainly pay her! Can't you do without a lady's maid? What could she do for you that you can't do yourself?'

'No! I need Allsop. Do you know how long it took me to train her? To teach her how I like things?' Her voice was harsh.

'For heaven's sake, Julia. You'll get her back in a few months, two at most.'

'Can you promise that? Can you? You told me that a year ago. And … and nothing's happened yet!' When he didn't respond, she said, 'You're exaggerating.' There was ill-concealed impatience in her voice. 'You'd put one of them out on the street, at Christmas?' Her eyebrows shot up in high, winged arches. 'Clumsy, don't you think? There's really no need for me to tell you what people will say.'

'Not before Christmas. After it, you fool!' he said. 'Between Christmas and New Year, when everybody's got their minds on something else.'

Gracie was frozen rigid just inside the dressing-room door. She dared not move. A stray hair was tickling her nose, but if she put up her hand to brush it aside, she might also move the door and the shadows would change. If either of them happened to glance her way, they would fling open that door and reveal her presence. It wouldn't matter what she said, or how much was the truth, she would not be forgiven for having overheard. Of course, she could simply go home to Samuel and the children. They would be delighted to see her, and she would be delighted to see all of them. But that would not solve any of the problems here in this house, and that mattered. It would feel like a failure, a broken promise to someone who believed in her. And more than Millie, it would be letting Charlie down.

Perhaps that was the heaviest burden of being a mother. It was not the getting up in the night, cooking regular meals, even if rations were a little short. Or sorting out quarrels, fighting away their fears that scared you as well; keeping everything clean and reasonably tidy. No, the heaviest burden was when your children totally believed in you, and were not afraid of the darkness in the world because they trusted you to protect them. She would do almost anything not to break that trust.

The Harcourts were still arguing about Allsop.

'Be sensible, Julia!' urged Mr Harcourt. 'Use one of the other maids; Allsop is very expensive.'

'And will you let Walters go?' she challenged. 'I'm sure we could teach one of the maids to look after your clothes.'

'One of the maids? Don't be absurd!' He sounded horrified. 'You don't realise what—'

'Exactly!' she said triumphantly. 'You don't want a little girl doing it, and you don't want your valet, who knows more of your private little habits than I do, transferring his loyalty to someone else.'

'Nobody's going to employ a valet who spreads household secrets all over the city, you fool! If he'd tell on me, he'd be capable of telling on them, too.'

'Oh, yes? And you imagine he would think of that before he spoke? In the strictest confidence, of course,' she said sarcastically.

'Yes, I do!' he snapped back. 'And don't be so

naïve. Really, sometimes I think you are simple minded.'

'Allsop knows all sorts of tricks to make a woman look better,' Mrs Harcourt continued. 'Just little things, but they make a world of difference. Things I didn't teach her. Which means she learned them in service to Lady Barden. Which tells me a lot about Lady Barden, which I'm sure she would rather I didn't know.'

'And you didn't tell anyone, of course?' he said sarcastically.

'Certainly not! Just … one or two. As I felt it advantageous. Sometimes,' she added, 'I think you are terribly stupid!'

'Funny, I think that quite often about you,' he retorted. 'So, we keep Allsop. Then, who do we lose? I agree, sending away one of the young ones would save almost nothing. We can't do without Cook. Gracie, or whatever her name is, we aren't paying anyway. And we have to have a house maid. I can't see you racing around with a duster and mop. What about the housekeeper?'

'Who's going to oversee everything if she goes?' Mrs Harcourt asked. 'You?'

'All right, then, what do you suggest? I'm not

going to a moneylender, and the banks won't stretch any further. God knows, I've tried! We are up to our necks in debt, Julia. People are beginning to suspect it. We can't borrow any more.'

'I don't know. Ask your mother for a loan. She's supposed to have loads of money in the bank. Or was that a lie?' There was fear in her voice again, as well as anger. 'Or haven't you the courage to ask her?'

'Do you imagine I haven't tried?' His voice held disbelief.

'Then what did she say?'

'Economise.'

'In what, for heaven's sake?'

'Anything. Everything. No more good wine. No theatre, ballet, opera for a while. In fact, no dining out, or dinner parties at home.'

'That means becoming socially invisible!' she exclaimed. 'Of course, we could always have people to afternoon tea?' she suggested witheringly.

'It won't be for long. Just control yourself.' His voice was full of contempt.

Gracie could imagine the woman scowling at him through rising fury.

She heard the bedroom door slam. Had he gone?

Or both of them? Could she push the door a little bit and look? She moved the door an inch.

Then she heard the bang as Mrs Harcourt dropped her hairbrush. Gracie froze.

'Allsop!' Mrs Harcourt shouted. 'Allsop, where are you? What have you done with my white lace blouse?'

There were several moments of silence, then the bedroom door opened and closed.

Gracie hardly dared breathe. Had Mrs Harcourt left the room?

'Yes, ma'am.' It was Allsop's voice only feet away from where Gracie stood. 'I'll see what I can do.' Her footsteps came as far as the dressing-room door.

Gracie stepped backwards and almost tripped over her own feet.

The door swung open and Allsop stared at her with intense black eyes.

Gracie stared back.

Allsop drew in a deep breath, and turned round to face Mrs Harcourt. 'I'll find it and bring it to you, ma'am.'

'Be quick!'

Gracie heard the sound of the bedroom door opening and closing again. And then Allsop appeared, her brows raised, her black eyes sharp. 'Get out quickly,' she ordered. 'I don't know what on earth you are doing here, but your explanation had better be good.'

Gracie turned to point at the silk dress. 'I brought that up, and was hanging it when they came in.'

'Possibly,' Allsop said. 'Show me your hands'

Gracie held them up, empty.

'Go down the backstairs,' Allsop ordered, light from the bedroom behind her intensifying the near-black of her hair. 'And in the future, when you hang anything else, leave the door wide open. You might possibly see and hear a lot of things you would rather you did not. Being invisible isn't always an advantage.'

'Thank you, Miss Allsop,' Gracie said with profound sincerity.

Gracie was wide awake as soon as she heard Bessie knock on the door with the cup of tea she always brought. They said 'Good morning' and 'How are you?' as usual but, like Gracie, the girl seemed subdued.

Gracie washed and dressed, and went downstairs to breakfast. She had porridge, then a boiled egg, and toast and marmalade. Nobody commented, although Gracie did notice Cook looking across the table at Mrs Jenkins with raised eyebrows.

After breakfast, Gracie followed Mrs Jenkins to the housekeeper's sitting room where she could speak without being overheard.

'Yes, what is it, Gracie?' Mrs Jenkins asked.

'I don't want to trespass on anyone else's work.' She reminded herself that she must stay here, because she was certain now that there was something very seriously wrong, and whatever it was lay deeper than a temporary shortage of money.

'What had you in mind?' Mrs Jenkins asked curiously.

'I'd like to light a fire in the library, ma'am. And dust all the books. This time of year, with the cold and damp, they'll get mouldy. It would be a terrible loss to let them get damaged.'

Mrs Jenkins looked at her with raised eyebrows. 'Very well, do so.'

'Thank you, Mrs Jenkins.'

She started in the library, a room she had been in only once. Then, it had seemed cold and a little damp; today, even more so. It was miserable weather. The hard rain of yesterday evening had turned to sleet, and ice pellets rattled against the windows. There might well be snow for Christmas.

Shivering as she stood before the cold, grey hearth, she thought about how she had not exaggerated. Paper was subject to mould, and all the beautiful leather covers with their gold lettering would not protect the pages from the creeping moisture.

She went back to the scullery to collect newspaper and kindling wood to lay a fire, just a small one to warm the room. When she came back, she found Archie, the red-headed boot boy, standing in front of the bookshelf, eyes wide, mouth half open. He jumped when he heard her moving behind him.

'Oh!' He had been caught where he had no business, and she saw the fear in his face.

'Are you going to help me light the fire?' she asked him with a smile.

For an instant he froze, then he gulped. 'Yeah, I … I am.' He took a breath. 'What for, Miss Gracie? Ain't no one ever comes in here.'

'To keep it dry,' she answered. 'If it gets damp, the books will be damaged. Paper goes mouldy if it's wet, and you can't wash it out or get rid of it, at least not any way I know. It's wicked to destroy ideas, and … and memories.' She struggled to explain something too big to be grasped easily. 'There's history in these books, about all kinds of people. And dreams, ideas, and stories, lots of stories.'

He stared at her soberly. 'Can you read?'

'Yes, I can.'

He bit his lip. 'I can't.'

'Well, you have to learn. Nobody can till they're taught to.' What was she saying? She would be gone before this time next week. What ideas was she putting into the boy's head? It was totally unfair. But how could she take it back now?

'You can read? Really?' He turned and pointed to a red book with gold lettering. 'What does that say?'

She leaned closer for a better look. '*The Decline and Fall of the Roman Empire*,' she read.

'What's that?'

'Too big,' she replied, and searched further along the shelf. '*Treasure Island*,' she said. 'By Robert Louis Stevenson. I've heard that it's a story of a boy who goes to sea in a big ship, and it's got a sailor in it called Long John Silver, who has only one leg. And there are pirates, and treasure, and all sorts of things.'

'Have you read it?' he asked, with the same awe he might have had if she had told him she'd gone to sea herself and found a treasure. But then perhaps, in a way, everyone who could read had done that.

'No,' she said. 'But maybe one day I'll get it for my sons to read.' That was not impossible. Then she saw his face and realised the mistake she had made. No one was going to read to him. 'Of course,' she went on, 'you could read it yourself, and then even go to sea, if you wanted to.'

'Could I?' His eyes were wide. 'I think I'd like that.'

'It's hard work,' she warned.

'Harder than being a footman?'

'I don't know,' Gracie admitted. 'More dangerous, like …' She stopped.

He frowned. 'Is that bad?'

'Not really, I suppose. But if you learn to read, you can go anywhere in your mind, anywhere real, or not real.'

'What do you mean, not real?'

'Magic worlds, like in *Alice in Wonderland*, that kind of place.'

'I never heard o' that.'

She was in too deeply now to find a way out. 'Well, Archie, if you learn to read, when you get time off, like on Sundays, you can go anywhere at all. You've got to learn to read.'

'How can I do that?' The light faded out of his face.

'Don't know.' She took a deep breath. 'But we'll find a way.'

'Is it difficult?'

'Not if you go bit by bit.'

'Mary wants to read, too. She wants to be a real cook, like our Cook, in the kitchen. But you have to read to do that. What to put in, all those things, and it's all writ down. That's so you do it right and don't forget how.'

Mary had a lot of auburn in her hair, but not bright red like Archie's, though his eyes were exactly the same clear violet blue.

'Is Mary your sister?' Gracie asked suddenly.

He nodded. 'Yeah, that's why she bosses me around.'

If Mary was thirteen, then how old was Archie? He wasn't thirteen as well. They might be twins, but she did not think so. 'How old are you, Archie?'

He blushed and avoided her eyes.

'Is she older than you?'

He nodded.

'How old are you?' she asked again, this time quietly.

He took a deep breath, but said nothing.

'Archie?' she said gently.

'Twelve, I think.'

'Really?'

'Eleven.'

She wanted to put her arm around him, but that would be an indignity he would resent. And if he didn't, maybe that would be even worse. He didn't have anyone, and he wouldn't have. Not now. And if Mr Harcourt put them out on the street, he might not even have Mary.

He was looking at her. She must say something, the right thing. 'Lots of time yet,' she answered, smiling at him. 'We'd better get this fire laid, or we'll both be in trouble.'

'Are you goin' to stay here, miss?'

The lift of hope in his voice cut her like a knife. She was tempted to lie. It would be so easy. 'For a little while. But I was older than you are, much older, when I learned to read and write, and when I spoke as if I knew what I was talking about. Now, help me clean out that grate and roll these papers up so we can get a fire started.'

He gave her a shy smile, then turned away and started on the newspapers.

\*

Gracie was in the main hall when she heard the sound of voices raised. What was going on upstairs? What was the quarrel between Mr Harcourt and his wife about this time? Was it anything more than fear, because the money was short? They both seemed to expect that something was going to happen quite soon to relieve them of that difficulty. Gracie did not know much of how the gentry came by their money. Did they rent out property? Some owned land, farms and so on, and of course that would bring in money, come harvest time. But that was over long before Christmas. Perhaps Mr Harcourt traded goods in and out of the country? When his ship landed, there would be a lot of money, if it was all safe. It did not matter. Once it came, whatever it was, they would be all right.

But it was hard, them burdening everybody else in the house with their difficulties. Charlotte Pitt had seemed to think that real gentry never burdened other people with their troubles. The main goal, what counted most, was that the Harcourts didn't put anybody out in the street … yet!

Gracie was going upstairs with towels. They always took a bit longer to dry than sheets. When she reached the west-wing landing, she saw Walters and Nora standing close together just outside the linen cupboard. The expression on their faces, the angles of their bodies, said it all. For a moment, they were unaware of the rest of the household, only of each other. He could not kiss her – that was too dangerous. Gracie understood the risk. They all knew that a slip would be used as an excuse to dismiss them. It would probably be Nora who would go, whether it was her fault or not. Gracie had heard Mr Harcourt say why he would not send Walters away. The man knew too many of Mr Harcourt's petty vanities. And it was only too apparent that Mr Harcourt himself was aware of them. And perhaps Walters was good at his job; Gracie had no idea. There had never been a male servant in the Pitt household. But then, Thomas Pitt had never particularly cared how he looked, and this was despite having risen to the top of his profession, which he had done after Gracie left to marry Samuel Tellman.

In earlier days, she had thought Tellman very grim. Indeed, until she had agreed to marry him, he had been a miserable man a lot of the time. Perhaps it was a mixture of the sights he saw, the people he had to deal with, the sadness and the poverty of too many, and above all the injustices he could not mend. And he had not liked Pitt much either, in their earliest days. That had changed completely. All of it. Samuel was good at his job, and Pitt had appreciated that, and told him so. Over time that had made all the difference.

But she had been happy working for the Pitts, and she had felt no desire to get married. Or have to start worrying about a roof over her head, what to eat, bills mounting up. And, quite honestly, she loved being part of Charlotte's life, and helping her to solve Pitt's cases. It was exciting, dangerous, and thrilling when they worked it all out. She had to love Samuel Tellman a lot before she was able to give that up! Now, she thought with a smile, how infinitely that had been worth it.

Little Charlie was hard work, often a worry, and ran Gracie ragged at times, as did Tommy and Vic, but she would not have changed that for anything! All the mysteries in the world were other people's problems now.

Except this one. What was wrong in this house? What did everyone feel so bad about? Was it fear? Or guilt? Or perhaps it was both.

She was undecided whether to warn the couple of her presence, but then walked past without even glancing at them. She pretended not to notice them, and they pretended not to notice her, although they surely must have. If they didn't take heed of people passing by, they were very quickly going to get caught.

Gracie came to the linen cupboard and put the towels away, then took another spare pillowcase to replace the one in Mrs Harcourt's bedroom. She liked a clean one every night.

The dressing room was open and Allsop was hanging up clothes. She was holding one of Mrs Harcourt's evening gowns. It was flame red, magnificently daring and beautiful.

'Oh, golly!' Gracie let out her breath.

Allsop stared at her, over the shoulder of the gown. It would have looked far better on her than on Mrs Harcourt. She had a dramatic face, severe, and her body was far too thin to be feminine. She was in her late thirties, at least ten years younger than Mrs Harcourt, but in her own, almost exotic, way she was strangely beautiful.

Allsop turned round and placed the dress on the rail in the wardrobe. 'Do you want something, Gracie?' she said a bit sharply.

Gracie ignored the question. 'I've never seen a dress like that. It's … beautiful.'

Allsop froze, then turned back slowly. For seconds

she did not speak, then she looked at Gracie curiously. 'Do you see a lot of dresses?'

'I used to, when I worked for Lady Pitt,' Gracie replied. It was stretching the truth a little, but she did like to look at the fashion in the *Illustrated London News*.

'I thought Cook said you were raised—'

'So I was.' Gracie was annoyed. 'I don't mean I'm going to wear a dress like that. But it doesn't mean I can't admire it. I don't suppose you'll wear it, either. And that doesn't mean you wouldn't look better in it than most of them.'

Allsop's pale face suddenly flushed with colour. 'Do you … do you think so? Well, you'd better not say that.'

'I won't.' Gracie shook her head. 'I've got more sense.' She walked a little closer and put out her hand to touch the shining fabric gently.

'It's silk,' Allsop said quietly. 'It's not just that it feels good, it drapes perfectly.' She smiled, and pointed to a diagonal seam. 'One side is cut on the bias. Do you know what that is?' She pulled it gently. 'It's not on the straight, it's a cross weave. See how it falls?' She demonstrated how the fabric fell more softly. 'Feel it.'

Gracie put her hand on the cross weave and felt it give gently. The difference was obvious immediately. She looked up at Allsop. 'Did you make it? This dress?'

Allsop smiled slowly, almost shyly. 'Yes.'

'I brought one up before, and it was beautiful, too. I couldn't have worn it. It would be wasted on someone as small as I am.' She refused to own the word 'short'. 'And I have nowhere to go in it,' she added, in case Allsop thought she was giving herself airs. She looked over Allsop's shoulder for a moment, at another dress, which was brilliant white and heavily beaded. 'Did you make that one, too?'

Allsop turned to look at the dress, then back at Gracie. 'Yes.' She seemed about to add something more, then changed her mind.

Gracie was amazed, and then angry that someone with such skill should profit nothing from it, except the occasional words, perhaps more than she knew, that went on in private. But Allsop was still a servant, at Mrs Harcourt's beck and call. And, of course, with dismissal hanging over her head, as it did everyone's in this house. No wonder Mrs Harcourt had refused to let Allsop go. It was for a great deal more than the possibility of her gossiping about domestic and personal secrets. Did Mr Harcourt know how many exquisite gowns Allsop had made for his wife?

'Do you copy them from somewhere or just make them up yourself?' It might have been an impertinent question, but it was out of Gracie's mouth before she thought about the politeness of it.

'I designed this myself,' Allsop replied. 'No lady wants to wear a gown that's a copy of somebody else's.'

'Mrs Harcourt must be the envy of every other lady of fashion.'

Allsop smiled, almost shyly. It gave her face a sudden softness far from its usual severity. 'I hope so.'

'You should be a dress designer, professional,' Gracie said sincerely. 'Get paid proper, and not do anything else. And have everyone know it was you who designed them.'

Allsop shook herself almost imperceptibly, as if wakening up to reality. 'I'm a servant,' she said grimly. 'Servants don't set up business by themselves. Costs money. Lots of it. It needs a place to sew, money to buy fabrics, and a reputation so people come to you.'

'People do set up, and do well,' Gracie said. 'And many not as clever as you.'

'But with more money, and a reputation. Don't be foolish. I know you mean well, but it's not possible. I haven't got time to stand around daydreaming, and neither have you. If you haven't got something to do, I'll find you something!' There was a challenging look on her face. It was as if she must resume normality. She hesitated just long enough for Gracie to guess that she very much indeed wanted this to be kept secret, but was uncertain whether to threaten or to plead.

Gracie must make that decision for her. She would not have betrayed such a confidence; it would be a cruel and grubby thing to do. She needed Allsop as an ally, not an enemy. 'We've all got dreams,' she said. 'That's what makes us go on. Ever onwards, I reckon. Even dogs dream. You know?'

Allsop looked extremely sceptical, as if she thought Gracie might be making fun of her.

'You look at them when they're asleep,' Gracie continued. 'You can see their legs twitching, as if they're chasing rabbits or something.'

Allsop smiled. It lit her face and for a moment she looked gentler, as if she were remembering a different, happier time when dreams were still within reach. 'I remember that; you're quite right. But you must still get back to work, and so must I.'

The next encounter of the day was after supper, and seemed hauntingly like an earlier one that still hung heavily in Gracie's mind. She went into the larder next to the kitchen and found Bessie, the between-stairs maid, cutting a huge slice of lemon curd pie, with cream on top. She froze when Gracie came in and saw the dish, complete with spoon, in her hand.

Gracie had to say something. If the child – and she was a child – were caught doing this again, she would be dismissed.

'You don't learn, do you?' Gracie said angrily. 'If you're still hungry, ask Cook for another slice of bread and jam. Put that back, and I'll say nothing, but you've got to stop! They really will throw you out! They weren't just threatening.'

The girl remained unmoving.

'Bessie, don't you understand?' Gracie said sharply. 'They'll put you out into the street, where it's cold and getting worse. It's wet and dark and dangerous. And there will be nothing at all to eat. Do you want that?' She felt horrible, standing in this pantry full

of food, with a hungry child, and intentionally terri-
fying her. But how else could she prevent her from
bringing about her own destruction? If they put her
out, Gracie would have to go with her, and take her
to her own house, until she could find somewhere
else for her. But all the people Bessie knew were
here, in this house. And, presumably, it was her home.
Where was her family? They could be anywhere.
And if they could have kept her, they wouldn't have
sent her to London, where she was clearly unfit for
this work. 'Bessie!'

'Yes, miss?'

'If you're still hungry, tell Cook, and she will get
something for you. Do you want me to go with you?'

'No, miss.'

'Why not? I'll explain to her that you're still
hungry.'

Bessie's voice was very quiet. 'It isn't for me,
miss.'

'No?' Gracie did not believe her for a moment,
and was disappointed that the girl would try to lie,
and get out of it. 'Again, who is it for?' Was she
going to blame someone else? Surely none of the
other servants would stoop low enough to get a child
to steal on their behalf? That was a hideous thought.

'For 'er upstairs, miss. She don't get much.' The tears were sliding down her cheeks now. 'Only ... only enough to keep 'er alive, no more.'

'Her ... upstairs?' Gracie repeated.

'Please, miss, I ain't supposed to say anything. Don't tell anyone, please.'

'Tell who?'

'The mistress, Mrs Harcourt.'

'I'll tell Cook.'

'She knows.'

'Cook knows that you are taking food? Really, the best food?'

Bessie nodded. 'Yeah.'

Gracie stared at her, and for the first time considered that the girl might be telling the truth. Could Cook be letting her take treats, like the pie, and the cream? 'Even the cream?' she pressed.

'Yes. Please, miss, let me go now, or I'll get caught on the way up.'

'Up ... where?' Gracie asked. She imagined the girl meant her own room, probably shared with Mary.

'Up to the old lady, miss.' Bessie blinked as her eyes filled with tears. 'I wish you wouldn't ask me.'

The old lady. Who on earth was she talking about?

But the girl was so close to tears Gracie did not ask. 'All right. Do you want any help?'

'No. I daresn't. If I'm careful, I won't get caught.'

'I'll stay here and make …' She was going to say that she would make sure none of the other staff followed too closely. Then she realised that Bessie was not doing this alone. Probably the other staff knew, too. But knew what? That young girls were taking treats up- and downstairs for some old lady? And that some of them, at least, were party to it?

She watched Bessie as long as she could, until she disappeared out of sight at the turn of the backstairs and up the next flight. Then she went back to the last of her own tasks for the day.

Who was the old lady upstairs? Did all the staff know about her? Was that part of what Millie was afraid of? Why hadn't she said so? Was it so dark a secret? Or was it even possible she did not know? Was it some servant too old to work? Or even a member of the family, secretly locked away because she was mad, and no one cared enough to send her to a regular madhouse? Or perhaps it was shame that kept her situation private. As a child, Gracie had heard about these terrible places, these asylums. The big one in London was called Bethlem Royal

Hospital, but it was referred to as Bedlam, because of the constant shrieks and howls of the people kept chained inside. Or so they said. She did not want to know about anybody having been there, and then coming out to tell about it.

Perhaps it was better to keep someone locked in an attic of their own house. But it was still a horrible thought. Maybe it was fear of insanity that held all of them in its grip.

That made sense. It would explain why everyone was so tense, frightened, even acting as if they were guilty of something. It was because they were aware of someone suffering, and they could do nothing about it. No one could do anything about it.

Gracie did not sleep well that night. She was affected by the deep anxiety and fear that Millie had tried to convey when she had come to her for help. Only now it was not an aimless thing, possible to dismiss as a mood, or a fancy that would pass. There was all the difference in the world between imagination of something nameless, and the very real possibility of being dismissed from your position, your home, warmth, food, friendship, to walk the winter streets hungry, or even in danger, looking for the shelter of a doorway to sleep in. And with no character reference, what was the point in even seeking another position?

She slept on and off and was at last resting when Bessie came knocking on the door with her cup of tea.

The girl looked pale, which was just like any other day. She was used to fear. It was not a stranger to her.

'Thank you,' Gracie said with feeling. She took the tea and drank carefully from the cup, so as not to scald herself.

'You all right, miss?' Bessie asked anxiously. 'You look a bit pale.'

Gracie smiled at her. 'Yes, thank you. I just didn't sleep as well as usual. There's nothing wrong.' Well, nothing more than usual, but she did not say that.

Bessie flashed her a bright smile, perhaps meant as encouragement, and then went out of the door.

Gracie washed herself in cold water, and then dressed and finished her tea, taking the empty cup down with her to breakfast.

She ate a bowlful of Cook's excellent porridge and drank another cup of tea, but was all the time thinking of an old woman whom Bessie cared about so much, and whose existence was never spoken of.

As soon as they had finished their meal, everyone left the table for their respective duties.

Gracie's first attempt to go upstairs and find whoever it was in one of the attic rooms was foiled by Mrs Jenkins, who gave her a small job, but too hard for any of the younger maids. They had not yet been taught finer needlework, even the simple task of replacing the stitching on a lace tablecloth, just the thing a guest would notice. It had to be done flawlessly, so as to be indistinguishable from the original hand work, and the housekeeper knew that Gracie could do this.

She considered asking Mrs Jenkins about the person upstairs, whom the young girls were sneaking treats to, and why such a thing was necessary. She looked at Mrs Jenkins' tense face, and how her hair was drawn back unflatteringly tightly, and she decided against it. She was sure Mrs Jenkins knew, although perhaps 'suspected' would be more accurate. But if Mrs Jenkins knew, or suspected so acutely that it amounted to knowledge, why did she not feel compelled to act? That was what Gracie wanted to know. Why would that be? Because it might endanger them all? Was this the dread that Millie sensed? A family secret, or shame, that only the senior servants were supposed to know, of necessity, because they had to care for this old lady? Gracie could understand that, almost. No one wanted to make public the fact that they had a member of their family who was not sane.

Telling Gracie outright might bring about the very thing they were trying to avoid. And if Gracie made Mrs Jenkins admit that she knew, then she'd also have to admit why she had done nothing about it.

The second time she tried to get to the top floor was even less fortunate. She went up the backstairs as far as the second floor, then through to the main part of the house and on to the landing. She had got no more than twenty feet when she heard Mrs Harcourt's sharp voice behind her.

'Are you lost, or … what's your name? Gracie?'

Gracie was momentarily confused. If she said she was lost, after having been here several days, it would make her look extraordinarily foolish. It was a large home, but not large enough for that. But if she said she was not lost, where could she be going? This was not the way to the servants' bedrooms, including her own. She searched frantically for an excuse. She could not afford to anger Mrs Harcourt, or get caught in a lie either. 'I …' she began. She swallowed, more of a gulp. 'I dropped ... I lost a small button. I dropped it somewhere around here, and I haven't got another one like it. If I found it, I could sew it back on.'

'Really?' Mrs Harcourt's neat, sharp brows rose. 'A button off what?'

Gracie's mind raced. 'Off a piece of underwear.' She looked straight at Mrs Harcourt and met her eyes. She did not have to pretend embarrassment, or at least considerable discomfort.

'Then perhaps you should ...' She looked at Gracie's slender form and bit back the remark she had been about to make. 'Well, if you don't find it, you had better ask Allsop for another button. I'll ask her for you! Until then, a safety pin will be adequate. You don't appear to be in any immediate difficulty, so you had better get on with your work.'

Gracie drew breath to argue, saw the unflinching gaze in Mrs Harcourt's sharp, hazel eyes, and changed her mind. She thought of turning round and going down the backstairs, and then up again when the woman had gone wherever she intended, but she thought better of it. Besides, she was certain Mrs Harcourt was going to wait there until she observed Gracie's obedience.

Gracie went down the front stairs slowly. She must remember either to 'find' her button or ask Allsop for another. Not that there were any buttons on her underwear!

It was early afternoon when she was passing the butler's pantry and saw Mr Denning sitting upright at the table, making notes in a leather-bound book.

He looked up as she passed. 'Oh! Mrs Tellman.'

She stopped and turned. No one else had addressed her so formally, and for a moment it was startling. 'Yes, Mr Denning?'

'Are you on an errand at the moment?' He rose to his feet. 'There is something I need to say to you.'

She swallowed. Had Mrs Harcourt complained to him? Had she possibly thought that Gracie was not telling the truth? Even that she was a little above herself and needed to be taken down a step, or possibly even dismissed?

'Yes, Mr Denning?' She tried very hard to keep her voice level. If she was not dependent on the job and could escape so easily, yet was made to feel nervous simply by the butler stopping her, what must the others feel like? She had come to help them, particularly Millie. What if all she did was create more trouble?

'Sit down.' He indicated the other stool, opposite the one on which he had been sitting. The butler's pantry was quite generous in size, and with the usual amenities. Gracie had seen such rooms before, but only rarely. The Pitts did not often stay away from home and have occasion to take a servant with them.

Now she regarded the butler's pantry only briefly, noting the hob on which a kettle might be boiled to make tea, and at any hour a gentleman might want it. And of course, there was a table with drawers that locked, which served as a desk in which to keep the accounts other than those Mrs Jenkins kept for the kitchen and household linens. It also served as a worktable on which to polish all the household silver: the knives and forks, spoons, fish knives, serving spoons, carving knives, the silver cruet sets, the teapot, salvers for carrying things, and anything else that might need polishing at least once a week.

'Yes, Mr Denning?' she asked again.

He was not a big man. His fair hair looked at first glance thicker than it was, because of the unruly curl in it. She thought, quite irrelevantly, that he must have been nice-looking as a younger man. She had noticed that sometimes he walked with a slight limp. Rheumatism? He stood straight, shoulders back, head high. Perhaps he was an old soldier, and the limp was the result of a wound from some war. She wondered if he had fought overseas. What lands had he seen, which faraway places? Maybe the army was the reason he had no family.

At this moment, he seemed to be finding it difficult to broach whatever subject had prompted him to call her in. The tension was growing with every moment that passed. It was not her place to begin first, but she was going to have to, if he did not say something soon. Had he been told to dismiss her, and he was finding it hard to do? Perhaps he imagined he was putting her out into the street, in midwinter, just before Christmas.

'Mr Denning, if you have been asked to put me out, please don't blame anyone for that. But I'll be fine. Better me than anyone else. I have a home and a husband and family. I used to be a servant, but I'm not now.'

'I know,' he said quickly. 'That wasn't what I was going to say. But this is difficult. There is something you need to know. And it is my duty to tell you.' He gave what was almost a smile. He met her eyes for a moment, then looked down. It was obvious that he found this every bit as difficult as he had said. 'You are not the problem, Gracie. Although perhaps you are bringing it to a head. Which may be what Millie intended, and an inevitable outcome.'

Gracie felt suddenly cold in this warm, comfortable pantry. But she did not interrupt him.

He looked up. 'There is a great deal of trouble here. Please don't deny it, because it is true, and I am sure you are aware of it. If I don't warn you, you may unintentionally make it worse.'

'Yes, sir, but I don't understand it.' That was not completely true, and the moment the words were out of her mouth she regretted them. She felt certain Mr Denning was a very private man, very loyal, and this was difficult for him to say. She knew that he must have felt compelled to speak like this, or he would not. But why? What was it that hurt him so deeply?

'Were you a soldier, once?' She asked this because she believed it was somehow relevant. It was a battle of loyalties inside him. She saw it in the way he stood, trying to hide his limp; the way he placed everyone within their duty, and expected them to understand and obey, even those too young to have such self-control.

Now he looked startled. 'Why do you ask, Mrs—'

'You remind me of a soldier,' she replied. 'And I can see that you have loyalties.'

Colour spread up his face, self-consciousness at having his inner feelings so well perceived. 'Yes, I was,' he answered. 'But that has nothing to do with what I need to say to you. I know that you are here to fill Millie's place, let us say until Christmas Eve, when you will surely wish to be home with your children, and I hope Millie would wish to be back here with us, in her home.'

Gracie was certain he had nearly said 'family'. It was what he felt, and she knew this as surely as if he had said the words. 'Mr Denning, I'm doing what Millie asked me to do. At least, I set out to. Now, I don't know exactly what that is.' She leaned forward earnestly, momentarily forgetting that she was junior, temporary staff, and he was the butler. 'There's something wrong here. Everybody is scared, but nobody says why.'

He started to interrupt her, then changed his mind. She must be quick, before he lost patience with her. 'I was up in Mrs Harcourt's dressing room, hanging up her clothes, when she came into the bedroom. She was with her husband. They were already talking and said things I shouldn't have heard. That was before I could open the door and come out.'

He blinked. She could see in his face that he understood. Now she had come to the point where she must tell the truth, or back away from it altogether. In fact, run away from the battle. 'They both agreed that they are hard up,' she went on. 'And that they have to spend less on everything. One of the first things would be to dismiss some of the servants.' She saw his face blanch, as if she had confirmed what he was already most deeply afraid of. 'They can't get rid of you. What respectable household functions without a butler and a cook? And they dare not let the valet or the lady's maid go, because they have to appear well dressed. They also have to be careful, because these servants know too many secrets about them and—'

'They would never gossip!' he interrupted, anger hot in his face.

'I know they wouldn't,' she agreed. 'But the Harcourts don't know that.'

Understanding flared in his eyes, and he drew in breath to speak.

'And it's good they think so,' Gracie went on before

he could interrupt. 'It'll keep them from showing those staff out, where decency wouldn't.'

'But the young ones, they are little more than children, and they can't tell anything because they don't know anything!' he protested. 'And who would they tell? This is the only house they know. And we are their family now.' He was clearly aware of laying his emotions bare in front of another servant, a young woman he had known only a few days. But he had no alternative. 'They're ... family,' he finished. 'It's my responsibility, but ...' he swallowed hard, 'I fear I can't do it alone.' He was embarrassed, but he did not look away.

'They won't let the younger ones go because it costs them almost nothing to keep them.' Other words Gracie had overheard came to her memory. 'Mr Harcourt seemed to think it wouldn't last long. There was money coming in soon; I don't know what.' She stopped. She did not know what else to say, but there was a look of understanding in his face, and grief.

She waited. It seemed cruel to demand he tell her. He was going to, as soon as he came to terms with it.

Hurried footsteps sounded on the polished floor of the passageway. A woman's, swift and light, then

silence again. But it would not be long before
someone came to the butler's pantry, in the ordinary
course of their duties.

'Have you been upstairs, to the top of the house?'
he asked with sudden urgency. 'Do you know why
some of the girls take desserts with cream, special
pieces of cake?' His eyes were very steady on hers.
The question was far bigger than it seemed.

'No. I've tried, but Mrs Harcourt cut me off. I
didn't dare try again.'

'I think you should know, but you must be careful,'
he warned. 'Go up at six o'clock this evening. You
can take the tray up, instead of Mrs Jenkins. I shall
tell her.'

Gracie drew in her breath to ask him what she was
supposed to do, what he expected of her, but his
polite smile meant dismissal. Then she heard a
different swift, light footstep in the passage, and she
was on her feet by the time Allsop came to the door.

'Yes, Mr Denning,' Gracie said, facing the butler
as if she were unaware of the woman standing just
outside the doorway.

'Six o'clock, Gracie,' he repeated, also ignoring
Allsop.

'Yes, sir.' Gracie turned and came face to face with

Allsop. 'Good afternoon, Miss Allsop.' And as if it were not possible that Allsop had come looking for her, she walked smartly into the passage and headed towards the hallway and the stairs.

At six o'clock, Gracie went back to the butler's pantry and found Denning waiting for her. Without saying anything, he held the door open and then led the way along the passage, his feet creating a sharp, quick rhythm, although almost silent.

They arrived at the kitchen. It was a beautiful room that Gracie could admire, even for a moment, without wanting it for herself. It was far too big and, at the least, it needed a cook and a scullery maid. There were two ovens, a large hob with enough room for five or six pots to cook at once. The kitchen table, scrubbed clean by generations of kitchen maids, offered enough surface to chop vegetables and fruit, roll out pastry, cut bread, with space to refill salt, pepper and mustard pots, all at the same time.

The whole room was warm, even in this midwinter time of year.

Gracie took a moment to look around her. The walls were hung with many different types of objects. Only one of the walls was used for cabinets.

One held everyday china, another was where the high-quality porcelain was kept for special events. Yet another held the silver cutlery, including knives, forks, spoons, and such. Higher up were shelves for silver teapots, coffee pots, jugs for water and milk, as well as sugar bowls, each one with its own appropriate tongs for picking up lump sugar. There were flower vases of all shapes and designs. Some were forged from silver, a few from pewter, but most were hand-painted porcelain.

Last were the pots and pans, many of them made from copper, their exterior reflecting the gleam of gaslight.

Gracie saw strings of round onions hanging beside bunches of dried herbs.

In addition to Cook, this kitchen was large and busy enough to require a kitchen maid who could wash the dishes and scrub the expansive table, take out rubbish, peel and chop vegetables. There was also a good argument for a below-stairs maid, who could handle the little chores. Apparently, they were managing without one.

Gracie was happy with her own kitchen, small enough so she could manage everything herself. That included sweeping the floor in a matter of moments, and using few plates and bowls to serve everyone a full meal.

Cook was looking at her, and when she said nothing, the woman turned to Mr Denning.

'Gracie will take the tray upstairs,' he announced. He gave no explanation, and his voice indicated that he did not expect an argument.

Cook raised her eyebrows and, for a moment, looked steadily at the butler, and then nodded as if she understood. She stepped aside and indicated a tea tray sitting on the huge table.

The kettle began to whistle. Cook turned and removed it from the hob. She added some of the hot water to the teapot, tipped it out, and then put in the fresh leaves, followed by boiling water.

'Can you manage that?' she asked Gracie.

'Of course she can,' Denning answered, before Gracie could say anything.

Gracie had no choice but to pick up the tray carefully. It was as heavy as she had feared. She would have to balance it very well. It would be a major disaster if she dropped it. Or worse, tripped and fell with it.

She walked in short and careful steps through the kitchen, out of the door, and into the passageway.

She was aware of Denning a couple of steps behind her.

She had gone some distance, concentrating on keeping the tray level and spilling nothing, when Denning caught up and took the tray from her. 'I can—' she began.

'No, you can't,' he said firmly. 'Too much depends on this. I will carry it up to the door, and you can take it into the room.'

She did not argue. She was intensely grateful to him. The tray was not only heavy, but it was too wide for her arms to carry without risk of dropping it. 'Thank you,' she said, giving up graciously.

They went up the backstairs, so even if another servant saw them, neither Mr nor Mrs Harcourt would. Denning went ahead of her through the upstairs door from the servants' quarters leading to the main house, first making sure no one was on the landing. He shot her a look to make her wait. When he was certain there was no one about, he gestured her forward and led the way up the next flight. He passed the tray back to her, then knocked on one of the doors.

They waited side-by-side in silence.

Denning repeated the knock, and when there was

still no answer, and frowning with anxiety, he turned the handle and pushed the door open.

Gracie went inside slowly. It was a room close under the roof, without an ordinary window, but a large dormer window instead. It let in the light, but there was no view that one could see from the bed, except the sky and the steady grey clouds.

She saw the usual bedroom furniture: a chest of drawers, a wardrobe, and a dressing table with an old-fashioned, silver-backed mirror, and a silver-topped glass container. And, of course, a silver-backed hairbrush, this one thick with white hair. There was a very fine film of dust covering every surface.

Gracie's eyes were drawn to the big bed, which dominated the room. It was clearly intended for a far larger room, like those on the floor below. In it sat an old woman, very small, and with untidy white hair that, with a shampoo and a good, gentle brushing, would have been soft, even beautiful. The woman was propped up in the bed, but she looked confused, as if she had just woken up and was not sure where she was.

'Who are you?' she asked Gracie. 'I don't know you.' Her voice was querulous, and she was clearly frightened.

For a moment, Gracie was stunned, and then a wave of pity swept over her. She put the tray down, because it was heavy, but she did not move any closer to the old lady.

'My name is Gracie,' she explained. 'I've come for a week or so to take Millie's place. She has a cold. Not a bad one, but she needs to get over it. I might stay until Christmas Eve. She'll come back as soon as she's well.'

'Gracie, did you say?'

'Yes. May I pour you a cup of tea, ma'am?' She made no move towards the woman. She wanted permission. The woman was obviously frightened, and needed time to adjust to this new face. Gracie saw how she hesitated, uncertain of change, or of anyone she did not know.

Gracie glanced behind her. She was relieved to see that Mr Denning was still there.

He came forward and spoke very gently. 'Gracie wanted to bring you something you'd really like, Mrs Harcourt. Look!' He pointed to the dish of fresh apple pie and cream.

The woman looked at it, then at Gracie, and a slow, sweet smile spread across her face.

Gracie glanced at Denning, then at the old lady.

The other dish on the tray held a couple of slices of meat, as well as potatoes, carrots, and winter cabbage.

'Are you hungry?' she asked, smiling at the old lady. 'If you like, you can have the apple pie first?'

'Can I?'

It was a few seconds before Gracie realised she was asking permission. 'Of course you can!' she said quickly. 'You can do whatever you like.' She did not bother to ask Mr Denning if that was all right, because she had no intention of obeying him if he said differently. 'Would you like a little help, so the dish doesn't spill?'

The old lady nodded.

This time, Gracie turned to look at Denning. He nodded almost imperceptibly and then went out and closed the door behind him, so softly she barely heard the latch.

Very carefully, Gracie took a small spoonful of the apple pie and cream and offered it to old Mrs Harcourt. It was taken slowly at first, but by the third spoonful she was accepting it eagerly, and looking for the next one. Neither of them spoke, but their eyes met every time Gracie held up the spoon. Finally, fear vanished from the woman's face and a look of pleasure came into her eyes, even of trust.

When the pie was finished, Gracie surveyed the main meal. 'Would you like a little of this?'

The woman thought for a second or two. 'Just the cabbage, please,' she answered. 'I don't like carrots very much.'

'Any of the beef?' Gracie asked.

The old lady considered this long enough for Gracie to realise she did not really want it. She looked terribly fragile. And perhaps her teeth were brittle. It would take a lot of chewing. Did anyone know? Did anyone take care of her? She looked at her a little more closely, at her nightgown, which was very worn, crumpled, and in need of changing for a fresh one. She could see only the top and the sleeves, but they were not clean. She looked at the old lady's face and saw shame in it. Shame and embarrassment. She knew she was not clean.

Gracie could have wept for her, for the humiliation. Instead, she smiled sweetly and said, 'The roasted potatoes look good. Let's try some, shall we?'

Slowly, old Mrs Harcourt ate the potatoes and the cabbage, but declined the carrots. Gracie poured the tea last, so it would be hot in the cup. She tasted it herself to make sure it was not scalding. She held the cup so the old lady's shaking hands would not drop it. As she did this, she noticed that there were food stains and marks of spilled tea on the sheets. In fact, the old lady herself smelled musty and a little sour.

When the meal was finished, Gracie took the tray and set it on the landing. She went back into the room and closed the door behind her.

The old lady looked puzzled, as if this was not what she had expected. 'Have I done something wrong?' she asked, her eyes wide with fear.

Gracie felt tears prickling her own eyes. 'No, of course you haven't,' she blurted out, the words filled with horror. 'Of course you haven't,' she repeated, her voice softer. 'I think that we need some privacy for one or two little … jobs. Does the bed not feel a bit uncomfortable? I can remake it …'

The old lady stared at her without answering. Was it fear? Or humiliation because she knew she was not clean, and this strange young woman was going to do something, and she had very little idea what it would be?

Gracie stopped at the end of the bed, keeping a good distance between them. 'I thought it would be a good chance to change your bed. Wouldn't you like clean sheets? A fresh pillowcase?'

For several seconds, there was no answer, and then the woman shook her head slowly. 'I … I don't know.'

'A fresh nightgown?' Gracie suggested. 'Clean and fresh? I like to have one every so often.'

The old lady smiled very slowly. 'Can I?'

'Certainly!' Gracie moved to make a place on a nearby chair where the old lady could sit and be comfortable.

Gracie wanted to change the bed first. She held out her hands and walked slowly towards the woman. 'Here, let me help you.'

'Oh!' the old lady declared, as tears filled her eyes.

Gracie stopped. What was she so afraid of? 'I won't hurt you,' she said. Very gently, a few inches at a time, she moved closer until she was right beside the edge of the bed. As she reached out, the old lady shrank into herself. 'I'm not going to hurt you,' Gracie repeated, this time her voice a whisper.

The old lady lowered her head, as if giving up the battle.

Gracie touched her arm, as thin as a child's. She was as small as Gracie, but not as strong. Gracie half lifted her towards the edge of the bed, helped her to gain her balance, then eased her to her own feet. She was as light as a child. Not much heavier than Charlie, who was not yet six years old.

Gracie understood that the old lady was not afraid; she was embarrassed and ashamed. She was not clean. She had needed help to go to the toilet and had not received it. Gracie was certain that this was what she was afraid of: being shamed in front of a new person who would not realise that this was something beyond her control, and it was distressing her more than the weakness, or any pain. It was a loss of dignity, robbing her of her last vestige of self.

Very gently, Gracie helped her to sit on the chair, a sheet wrapped around her, both for warmth and for dignity.

'You just sit there,' she told her gently. 'I'll get you some clean linen and take away this to wash. Don't move, please. I wouldn't like you to fall.'

The old lady nodded obediently.

Gracie gathered up the soiled sheets, folding the unclean parts inside so they were invisible. She would deal with the nightgown later. She must collect a clean one, and get a bowl of hot water so she could bathe the old lady.

'I'll be back in a minute or two,' she promised, and added, 'please God' under her breath. She hurried out of the door, closing it quietly behind her, then along the passage, looking to see there was no one visible before going down the stairs, running to the door at the backstairs, and then down to the laundry. She wasn't going to wash the sheets now; it was a long job. They would have to be rinsed first. That she could do, and would do, as a matter of decency. When one is old, or ill, a lot of things were not easy: sleep, strength, freedom from pain. But everyone could have dignity.

She left the sheets and pillow slips in one of the large tubs for bed linens and towels, and then rushed upstairs to find clean sheets and slips. She picked up two clean towels as well, so big she could not carry them and see over the top, so she moved slowly.

'Where are you going with those?' It was Mrs Jenkins. 'You are not due clean sheets yet, and certainly not two towels that size!'

Gracie's mind raced. Mrs Jenkins knew about the old lady upstairs. About her condition. She was not insane at all, merely old, and a little confused and forgetful, but left alone, ignored except for being given enough food to stay alive. Why? Clearly Mr Denning knew, and Mrs Jenkins and Cook. What prevented them from sending someone up to change the bed linen more often? The sheets she had just removed were weeks old. Why? Who were they protecting? Themselves? Everyone's home and future? And yet Denning knew, and he had intentionally taken Gracie upstairs to the room. Why? Because he didn't care if Gracie was thrown out? Or because he knew she wouldn't be? Or maybe he wanted her to do something about it. She was free in a way the rest of the household was not.

But why? The old lady must be Mr Harcourt's mother. Why was she kept in an attic, away from her family, even from public view?

'Gracie!' Mrs Jenkins said sharply, interrupting Gracie's thoughts.

With both anger and pity, Gracie answered, 'To change the old lady's bed. It's filthy! It needs doing every other day, not every other week.'

Mrs Jenkins froze. The struggle in her face was clear, a mixture of anger, guilt and pity. She must have been torn between letting one of the young girls take responsibility and being dismissed, and taking it herself. And if she were dismissed, who would look after the girls?

Gracie realised that she herself was the only one

who was not hostage to fortune. Her safety, her home, her survival did not depend on keeping this job. The worst anyone could do was send her home to her husband and children. They could not threaten her with a bad character reference, or none. She had no need for it. 'I will take care of it, Mrs Jenkins,' she said quietly. 'And I will see to the laundry.'

Mrs Jenkins stared at her. 'Do you know what you are doing, Gracie? If Mrs Harcourt catches you, what do you intend to say to her?'

To Gracie, the answer was obvious. 'That I did not ask you, and you had no idea that I had taken it upon myself to attend to what I saw as a need. Nor did I consult Cook or Mr Denning.'

Mrs Jenkins breathed in and out. 'I see. At least, I think I do.' Her expression softened. 'Please, be careful.'

Gracie nodded, and then hurried past her and on up the stairs. She was tempted to look back, but it was better that she did not. She had told her the truth. The longer she thought of it, the more certain she was that, one way or another, Millie had come for her because she was the one person who could try to do something. No one else could! Millie was exhausted and she could certainly do with a few days away from Harcourt House. She might not be suffering the head cold Gracie had invented, but she was sick with worry.

Gracie was not angry, nor was she offended. In fact, she accepted the mission with a sense of dedication. She gripped the clean sheets more tightly and raised her chin as she went up the final flight of stairs.

Back in the bedroom, she found the old lady sitting in the chair exactly where she had left her, her arms held tightly around herself. She was staring at the door.

'Hello,' she said uncertainly. She was almost like a child expecting to be struck for some offence she did not understand.

Gracie smiled at her. 'Would you be all right in the chair for a few minutes more, while I make the bed?'

'Yes.'

Gracie shook the clean sheets out, letting them open up and spread across the bed. She moved round quickly, tucking in corners and pulling it tight, all the time talking to the old lady to take her mind off the fact that she was sitting in a thin, soiled nightgown while a young woman she barely knew was making her bed up. Gracie told her about her own family, Charlie and Tommy and Vic.

'Charlie's my eldest,' she said conversationally, as if the old lady had asked. 'She's nearly six. Mind, she has been saying that since she was five and a half.'

When it was smooth all over, she opened the second sheet, and tucked it in at the bottom only.

'Does she look like you?' the old lady asked.

Gracie thought for a moment. 'I reckon she does, a bit. I hope she doesn't grow up to look like my husband.' Samuel's lean face came sharply to her mind, with its lantern jaw and steady eyes. 'That would be too much like a man.'

Then she looked around for the two blankets that were on it before. She was surprised to find the lightness of the first one. There was no weight, no fluffiness or warmth. It felt as if it had been too long used, washed and worn thin. The second was not much different. 'Don't you get cold at night?' she asked. Without awaiting a response, she went on talking. 'When they were tiny, Tommy and Vic looked a lot alike, but now that they're bigger, they are getting to look different. Vic, he's the youngest, his hair is getting darker all the time, while I think

Tommy's is going to curl. Don't know where he got that from.'

The old lady smiled, as if she were imagining him.

Gracie looked at the bedding in her hands. 'I'll find you another blanket. Or, better still, a quilt. That wouldn't be so heavy.'

'How could you do that?' the woman asked.

'I think I saw something in the linen cupboard,' Gracie replied. 'I'll just go and look, see what I can find.' She gave the old lady a quick, bright smile, then went out of the door and downstairs to the linen cupboard as quickly as she could. If there were no blankets in the cupboard, where else could she look? And what excuse would she give if stopped by anyone other than Mr Denning?

As it turned out, she passed only Archie, carrying boots down to where they could be polished, without being afraid of getting shoe polish on the floor, carpet or the clean wood of the kitchen table. He gave her a cheeky grin, which she surprised herself by returning. It was like a beam of sunlight through a slow, deep-soaking rain.

There were no blankets in the linen cupboard. Nor was there anything else she could use to make old Mrs Harcourt more comfortable. What else could she find? The curtains in the old lady's room were thin: they barely shut out the light, never mind the air off the cold glass. A frost would feel as if it were inside! Gracie had been in a room once where there was ice on the inside of a window. Good curtains would keep any warmth inside! Were there any others? Some households have summer and winter curtains. Even a lining would make a world of difference. And that carpet. There was only a thin mat on the old lady's floor. Surely there was a larger, thicker floor rug somewhere that could be used? And better pillows as well, possibly ones of a pretty colour.

She returned to old Mrs Harcourt and helped her back into the bed, then excused herself to look for the other things she needed. This was the only room the old lady saw. It should have something pretty in it, something bright and soft.

It took her far longer than she had intended, but finally, with Bessie's help, she went back upstairs with one softer, plumper pillow. It felt a lot better but had only a plain case. She had failed to find a pretty one. But she did have an old rug that was a lot thicker than the one there now, and had a nice red pattern on it. She also failed with the curtains, so she took one of the blankets from her own bed.

For the remaining nights she would survive without that blanket. Instead, she would take the blanket she had and roll it around herself until she was inside three layers of it. She had no extra layer of flesh, never had had, but she was young, and she was not going to be there much longer.

Then she went back upstairs, with Bessie helping her carry the new things. Gracie did not explain any of it to her. It wasn't necessary. She would have to have done this before, but she would have been dismissed if she were caught, and she knew it. Anyone who had helped would run the same risk.

'Ain't you afraid, miss?' the girl asked in awe.

'No, I'm not,' Gracie replied. 'If this were my house or my food on the table, and I was afraid of being thrown out, maybe I wouldn't be doing it. But the truth is, if they throw me out, I'll just go to my own house. But I don't think that, because I have things to do here. But you need to do what I tell you, so they won't do anything to you.'

'I want to do it, but ...' She said it firmly, but she didn't have the words to finish the thought.

'I know,' Gracie said, saving her the trouble of trying to explain.

Bessie understood and she followed on Gracie's heels, her arms overflowing. 'That's why I took the pudding,' Bessie said.

'I know,' Gracie answered. 'And it needed courage.'

They arrived at the bedroom. Gracie opened the door and they both went in, dropping their loads of bright things on the floor.

The old lady was still sitting as Gracie had left her. She looked startled. It took her a moment or two to remember who Gracie was, and dismiss her first reaction of fear. Bessie, she knew immediately.

'Hello, Grandma,' Bessie said with a shy smile. 'This time, I'm here 'cause I'm allowed. Least, I think so.' She glanced sideways at Gracie.

'Certainly, you are,' Gracie assured her. 'Now, let's finish the bed with these clean things, and get Grandma comfortable. But, Bessie …' she took a deep breath, 'could you help me give Grandma a bed bath?'

Bessie looked confused. 'A … what?'

'A bed bath.' Gracie did not know for sure if that was the right word for it, but she had been present when one had been given in a hospital, during the occasion of a visit. The memory came back sharply now. 'It's hard to keep someone clean and comfortable

113

when they are not well enough to get safely into a proper bathtub.'

Bessie's eyes widened. 'Yeah? I'll do that.'

It was a long task. They had to ask Walters to fetch more hot water upstairs in two pails, twice. He had no idea what they were going to use it for, but he was happy to help. Of course, he left immediately.

Bessie helped Gracie lift the old lady very gently on to the towel spread across the bed, then take off her soiled nightgown and put it out of sight. They had another towel over her and then they uncovered her one part at a time, and as gently and quickly as possible, washed away the ingrained dirt and soil of weeks, perhaps longer.

And all the time Gracie kept talking to the old lady, to keep her mind off the indignity of having servants wash her body. 'Charlie will be telling Samuel what to do, because she watches me all the time. Children do that, even when you don't know it.' She smiled. 'I know that I wag my finger when I'm telling them off for something. The other day I saw Charlie do exactly the same thing to Vic. It was like looking in a mirror and seeing myself!'

Gracie tried to keep her emotion out of her voice, but she was deeply moved by the state of the old lady's body. She was so light because there was barely any flesh on her bones. Her skin was not clean, but that was being gently remedied. She treated with tender care the places that were angry and red, but the bruises could not be so easily dealt with. Gracie thought how it must hurt to move. She told herself to hide her emotions, the rage inside making her want to punish someone, and with such intensity that they would never, as long as they lived, forget it; never stop having nightmares that it could happen to them someday, and no one would help them.

Gracie tried to think of happy things, funny things the children had said, the stories she had told them as they sat by the fire in the evenings.

'Of course, Vic kept going to sleep, and every time he woke up again Tommy had to tell him what he'd missed. You never heard such a story in your life, as it turned out in the end!'

'But happy?' the old lady asked.

'Oh, of course. You have to send them to bed believing it'll all turn out right in the end.'

Did you? That's not how it worked out in life. But you don't tell a three- or four-year-old that. Or an almost-six-year-old. Although Charlie had asked one day, after a story that had changed rather a lot in the telling, 'Does it always come right in the end, Mam?' It had been late. Not the time to face truth and Charlie's inevitable string of questions. 'If you wait long enough,' she had said to the child.

'That's right,' the old lady agreed with a nod.

Finally, they finished, and the pails were taken away, the extra towels removed, and the old lady was sitting up in bed in a spotless, fresh nightgown. There was a new, thick rug on the floor, and a third blanket on the bed. Bessie left, saying she would come back with a fresh pot of tea in ten or fifteen minutes.

'There now,' Gracie said, smiling at the old lady. 'Just one thing more. Let's brush your hair, very gently. I won't hurt you, I promise.' When the old lady looked a little anxious, Gracie repeated, 'I promise. It will feel nice. May I?'

The old lady hesitated, then smiled. 'Yes, you may,' she said.

Gracie took the brush and, sitting next to the woman, she began to move the brush gently, trying to undo as many of the knots as she could before the brush caught on them and pulled them out.

Moments after Bessie returned, everything changed.

There was no knock. The door flew open so hard

it banged against the wall and swung back. Mr Harcourt stood in the entrance, his face purple-red with fury.

'What in God's name are you doing? Who told you that you could come in here?' he demanded. He stared at his mother, then back to Gracie 'How dare you? What have you done to her? I demand to know!' Before she could respond, he announced, 'You! Consider yourself fortunate I have not asked you to leave – yet!'

Gracie was far more furious than she was afraid. 'We washed her. Bessie did nothing except what I instructed her to do—'

'You instructed?' he cut across her, shouting her down. 'Who the hell do you think you are? You do not give instructions to anyone in this house. You are a temporary servant, for God's sake, and tomorrow you will be nothing. Whatever it is you do, someone else will fill in.'

'Gilbert …' the old lady started to speak.

'Be quiet!' he snapped.

She shrank back as if he had slapped her.

Bessie was so pale, Gracie thought she might faint.

Gracie's mind raced. Every instinct was to fight back. But if she did, would that make it worse for the rest of them? Above all, would it make it even worse for the old lady? That had to be her main thought. The others might escape, do better or worse, but they could survive it. But there was no escape for her. And without the servants, who would care for her? What would happen to her? The old lady knew this too well. New servants might not even know she was there. Certainly, they would not risk their jobs to take her apple pie and cream! If they took anything at all, with a new cook, it could be half their own meals.

She looked across at the old lady, shrinking back into the pillows behind her. There were tears on her cheeks, but she would not cry out against him, perhaps for the sake of those very servants.

Gracie was alone in that she could act independently, not for the safety and welfare of the others, but independently for herself. Harcourt could put her out on the street tonight, but she would simply go home! In fact, the thought tempted her for a moment. Then she looked at the old lady again, and at Bessie, and knew that was the coward's way out. She, of all of them, had the obligation to fight.

But there was no point if she had no chance of winning. If she lost, she might make it even worse for all of them, even for Millie when she came back. She must fight, but how?

Harcourt was staring at her. 'Get out!' he ordered, his face still flushed with anger, and now with something that could also have been fear.

What did he imagine they had done? And more important, what would he do to the old lady if there weren't others willing to help? He would do nothing physical, she believed, but what might he say to her? Whatever it was, she couldn't fight back. Nor would Bessie, even if she regarded the old lady as a grandmother, someone she loved and who loved her. That relationship was another thing that shouldn't be broken. Gracie urged herself to think. 'Mr Harcourt,' she started, then swallowed.

'What!' he snapped. 'What have you to say for yourself, then?'

'All we did was change the sheets, sir. They were no longer clean. And we got Mrs Harcourt a clean nightgown, that's all.'

'All?' he said, raising his eyebrows. 'You've been up here for hours! Gossiping?'

'No, sir, there's nothing to gossip about.' Gracie kept her temper with great difficulty. 'We just moved a little slower than usual, so we didn't hurt her, bruise her by mistake, or break her skin. She's very fragile, bruises easily if you're not careful.'

'I know how to touch my own mother, girl!'

'I'm sure you do, sir.' She did not lower her eyes from his. 'But it isn't fitting that you, as a gentleman, should bathe an old lady, even your mother. I think your respect for her wouldn't let you do that.'

His face flamed, but he could not think of any argument. The frustration was naked in his expression, and there was something else as well. Was it the beginning of shame?

'And nobody expects you to change the bed linen, sir,' she added. 'Would you like a cup of tea, sir?'

'What?' he demanded incredulously, his eyebrows rising alarmingly.

She met his eyes without flinching. 'You came up here to visit your mother, so I thought you might like to share a cup of tea with her. We can bring it up right away. And perhaps a piece of cake?'

The old lady choked back her tears. For a second her eyes were bright. Then she drew in a deep breath, and held it.

Gracie waited.

'Yes,' Mr Harcourt said at last. 'Bring it up, and some fruitcake.'

'Yes, sir,' Gracie said quietly. She looked at the old lady. 'Do you like fruitcake too, ma'am? Or would you prefer sponge cake?'

'I prefer sponge cake, please,' she replied. It was what Gracie had expected, since her teeth were too brittle for dried fruit.

'I'll be back in a few minutes,' Gracie promised. She smiled at the old lady. She wanted her to know that it was a promise, all of it: the tea, the cake, the clean bed.

'Thank you, dear,' the old lady said, with a sudden, wide smile.

Downstairs, in the kitchen, Gracie felt totally different. Her anger had disappeared, yet she found herself shaking as if she were exhausted, and ice cold inside. Samuel could not help. He had no right even to enter the house. There was no crime. He would jeopardise his own job, and then where would they all be? This was ridiculous! She had not been attacked, threatened, abused, nothing that endangered her at all. She had a safe, warm home she could go to, where she was both needed and loved. But few of the people here could say the same. And if she walked out, ran away, it would only make it worse for them, and for her. They would watch her go, and the darkness around them would close in even more tightly. And she would feel less of herself, as if she had left some part of her kindness behind. If there was one thing she had learned over the years, it was that she could not hide from herself.

Cook was looking at something in the oven. Straightening up, she closed the oven door and automatically placed her hand against her back.

'I think he might put me out,' Gracie said quietly. 'I changed the bed linen for the old lady. He came in and … I thought …'

'I know, love,' Cook answered, moving again to ease her back. 'You've got a nerve, and God bless you for it.'

'I might have done more bad than good for old Mrs Harcourt. I only did it to help! What's going to happen to her?'

Cook's face filled with sadness. 'I'd like to tell you she'll be all right, but she won't. She's a lot weaker than she used to be, poor soul. All we can do is give her the things she likes to eat, and wash her now and then. Bessie's good at that. She were raised by her grandma, and she took to the old lady. Risked getting caught to take up a treat for supper when she could.' She looked away. 'They called her a thief, and she never told them it were for the old lady, in case they took it out on her.'

'What are they trying to do? Starve her to death?' Gracie demanded.

'Maybe,' Cook replied, her eyes averted, watching what she was doing.

Gracie did not argue. She had seen just a glimpse of that bravery and kindness, and felt fear for Bessie. 'I admire Bessie for that,' she said quietly. 'And I told her so.'

Cook's eyebrows rose. 'You told her?'

'I think she deserved that. And I told her because I felt it.'

Cook's voice cut in, a trifle sharper. 'I suppose you didn't think how she might be encouraged by that? And go and do it again? She's a child, Gracie! She's looking to belong, to find a mother, a grandmother, too.' The woman breathed out slowly, shutting her eyes, and then spoke again, softly this time. 'Someone to talk to, to take treats to. Someone who listens to her, cares about her.' Her voice was thick with emotion. She opened her eyes suddenly and glared at Gracie. 'Don't you go getting her into trouble, talking without thinking first! As they put her out in the street, without a reference, are you going to find a place for her then? And if you do, will those new people care about her?'

Gracie felt pain and loss rise up inside her. Her mind raced. She could not let that happen, no matter what it cost. 'Yes,' she said, barely stopping to draw breath. 'If they throw her out, she can come to my house for Christmas. And after that, the lady I used to work for – and she is a lady, title and all – will find Bessie a position.'

Cook appeared somewhat mollified.

Gracie left the kitchen before any more questions could be asked. She passed Walters in the passageway.

He looked worried and he came to a stop, then turned round and faced her. 'I understand your anger, miss …' He hesitated, as if uncertain whether to call her by her surname or her Christian name. 'Mrs … Gracie. But be careful you don't try to rescue the old lady at the cost of everyone else. It's—'

She knew what he was trying to say. 'I understand,' she cut him off. 'I was so angry and I might have jumped in too quickly, but they left her like that.' What she did not say was, now that she had gone so far, she didn't want anyone to know the indignity of the old lady's state, most particularly reveal it to a manservant. It was humiliating, no matter how deeply he pitied the woman. But didn't the entire staff know? How could they not?

She was not sure whether he understood her or not, but she saw that he was biting back whatever he had been about to say. And there was intense pity in his eyes.

'Be careful,' he said quietly.

'I will, yes,' she agreed, then turned away from him and hurried on.

She went to the butler's pantry to report to Mr Denning. If she could work up the nerve, she would ask him if there was anything more she could do. She arrived at the door, which was not quite closed, and she knocked. No one responded, but she could hear Mrs Jenkins' voice from inside.

'She's out of control. She may mean well, Arthur, but she's going to get the younger ones thrown out into the street, beginning with Bessie. That child is so lonely, she'll take any kindness and play into it! She's too young to be away from home! They'll finish up in brothels, or worse. They don't know any different. Anyone who offers them food and a place to sleep will own them!' Her voice was rising sharply. 'You can't do it! The old lady hasn't got long.' Gracie heard the woman draw in her breath. 'We can't help everyone! If we don't choose, we'll lose them all!'

'She's thirteen.' Mr Denning's voice sounded hurt, desperate.

'Is she?' Mrs Jenkins demanded. 'I should say she's about eleven, like Archie.'

'So what if she is?' he replied.

Gracie could hear the weariness in his voice. This was clearly an argument they had had before. Not about the old lady, but about having to pare down the staff.

'She has nowhere else to go,' said Denning, his voice rising in exasperation. 'We are all the family she has.' His voice was thick with emotion. 'This time of the year she'd freeze to death in the street, and God knows who would take her in, or for what purpose.'

'I know that,' Mrs Jenkins said, making an effort to be gentler. Gracie could hear the strain in her voice. 'So, what are you going to do about Gracie? Her heart's in the right place, but she doesn't understand it here. There's no fear in her.'

'She's seen the old lady,' he began.

'I know that, too!' Mrs Jenkins' voice was shaking.

'But the old lady can't live much longer. She's as frail as a bird. Mary and Bessie and Archie, God bless them, are only children. You're not wise, Arthur. You know as well as I do what will happen to them if they're put on the street. They'll finish up in the gutter, or the grave.'

Gracie knew Mrs Jenkins was distraught when she repeated the argument she had made only minutes earlier, that anyone offering the children food and shelter would own them.

There was movement inside the butler's pantry, causing Gracie to step back from the doorway and walk quickly along the passage without looking back. She moved as silently as possible, so that if either Mrs Jenkins or Mr Denning came out, they would see her back disappearing, and would have no reason to suppose she had overheard them.

Had Millie known what was happening in this house? Was that why she had asked Gracie to take her place? She had pretended not to know. Gracie's anger at what might have been deliberate deception lasted only seconds. What else could the child do? Pit herself against them? Let it all happen, keeping her head in the air, in case she got caught … or hurt? Perhaps Millie desperately wanted not to be alone in the situation, as it gained speed towards what she feared would be the final disaster.

Was it inevitable? Really?

Who else could Millie have asked? Gracie was not sure. There was no one she distrusted, at least for honesty, but what about ability? Who could do anything that would effect a change? Millie had not leaned on any of them. Instead, she had come to Gracie.

It was the middle of the following afternoon when Walters opened the front door to the doctor and showed him into the sitting room, where young Mrs Harcourt was reading. Walters came back to the servants' dining room.

To Gracie's surprise, she realised he was looking for her. 'What is it?' she asked.

He looked uncomfortable, but not indecisive. 'Dr Bramwell has just called. Mrs Harcourt will take him up to see the old lady. Will you go with her, please?'

Gracie was startled. 'She asked for me? Why?' It was not meant as a refusal. In fact, she was glad to have the chance to be there, perhaps even to say something confidential to the doctor. But why had they asked for her? Because she was new, and temporary?

'No,' Walters replied grimly. 'I am the one asking you because you bathed her and saw how she really is. You can tell the doctor, and then the worst that can happen to you is that Mrs Harcourt will dismiss you. I'm sorry, but you have somewhere to go.'

It sounded like an apology, but she could see in his face that he was not going to take it back. She did not want him to. What he had said was true. And it was, in a way, an expression of trust.

'Does he know how ill she is?' she asked. 'I mean, does he just take their word for it?' Should she tell him what she knew?

'I don't know,' he answered before she could add any more. 'I don't think he wants to know. And ...' The colour washed up his face. 'Perhaps the old lady is too afraid, or too embarrassed, to tell him.'

Gracie's stomach knotted with rage and pain. This was beyond cruel! It was a slow, deliberate death. And Walters was asking her to help. She stood up. 'Yes, Mr Walters,' she said with a tiny smile. 'I'll go and wait in the hall, in case they want me.'

He nodded, with a hint of a smile.

Gracie had longer to wait than she expected, but finally Mrs Harcourt came out of the withdrawing room, immediately followed by a plump, fair-haired man with a beard greying in patches, and carrying a medical bag.

'Can I help, ma'am?' Gracie asked demurely. 'Towels or hot water for the doctor to wash his hands, maybe?'

'Oh, yes, thank you,' the doctor accepted, at the same time that Mrs Harcourt declined.

Gracie chose to hear the doctor, then swiftly ran in front of him to lead the way upstairs. On the first floor, she collected a bowl of hot water and a towel meant for the housemaid's room. And then, carrying them carefully, she followed after the doctor and Mrs Harcourt to the top floor. She went into the old lady's room, where Mrs Harcourt was standing on one side of the bed, and the doctor on the other. In between them, the old lady stared forward, her face white and frightened, until she saw Gracie, and then it lit up with a bright, relieved smile.

'Hello, dear,' she said quite clearly.

Gracie smiled back at her. 'Hello, ma'am,' she replied. She would like to have said more, but dared not in front of the young Mrs Harcourt, whose grim, tight-lipped expression reminded her who was in charge. Gracie would have to leave the house soon enough, and she was already, in the back of her mind, trying to think of a way to stay. Or perhaps come back straight after Christmas Day. She couldn't leave Samuel to have Christmas alone with the children. Being with them was her most important job, to make them happy, and for them to know that, whatever happened, she would never leave them.

Gracie put the bowl of hot water on the dressing table and the towel beside it. 'There you are, sir.' She kept the towel in her hands, to pass to him when he was ready.

Mrs Harcourt drew in her breath, probably to tell Gracie to go, but it would have been rude to the doctor, who was accepting her assistance, however slight. Perhaps she did not want to incur his anger or cause him to ask additional suspicious questions, on the chance that he did not know. But how could he not? Was he being paid for this? She put that thought out of her head.

The doctor washed his hands, then took the towel, dried them, and passed it back. 'Thank you,' he murmured, then turned his attention to the old lady.

Gracie stood almost motionless, hoping the doctor would engage Mrs Harcourt and forget a maid who was no more than a convenience.

But it was the old lady who broke the silence.

'Thank you for coming, Doctor. I'm feeling much better.' She drew breath to continue.

Gracie was terrified she was going to say something about how she and Bessie had changed the bed linen and brought her treats.

'Good,' the doctor said. 'The medicine is helping?'

The old lady did not even glance for a moment at Gracie. She looked at the doctor with a sweet smile. 'I don't know, Doctor. Have you changed my medicine? Do you suppose it is helping more than you expected?' She asked it innocently, as if that might be the answer.

He hesitated, perhaps caught between pointing out that there was no cure for age, and that any help would be only temporary. Had he any idea that she was being slowly starved to death? Or was it some illness that was wasting her away, and they had not told her because there was nothing they could do?

'Doctor, will it …?' young Mrs Harcourt began. Her expression was unreadable. Was she refusing to accept the truth, or indifferent to it?

'Thank you, Julia,' the old lady said. 'But don't disturb yourself. I am quite happy to take Dr Bramwell's advice. There is nothing to struggle for. I'm coming towards the end of life. All I want is to be as comfortable as I can. You've …' She smiled for a moment, not looking at anyone, then she glanced at Gracie and back at her daughter-in-law. 'I have attended to all the tedious sort of things that I have to.'

'You mean your will? I mean your affairs …?' The younger Mrs Harcourt ground to a halt, looking as if she wanted to continue, but could not find the words. Was it the doctor's opinion she feared? It surely was not Gracie's. Who would listen to a maid, anyway?

'Yes, Julia, my will is attended to. Actually, it has been for quite a while. And I knew very well what I was doing. Of sound mind, and all that.' She turned to the doctor. 'I am of sound mind, am I not, Dr Bramwell?'

'You most certainly are, Mrs Harcourt. Perfectly sound. In fact, you seem to be more yourself than you have been for some time.'

'I have one or two items I wish to make sure are specifically left to Julia.' She looked at her daughter-in-law. 'I just want to be certain,' she added with a frown. 'Julia, you cannot witness this, because it concerns you.'

'Of course, Mother-in-law,' Julia said with evident

pleasure. The tight lines of tension eased out of her face. She turned and walked out of the room, passing Gracie as if she were a piece of furniture. Her footsteps could be heard down the uncarpeted corridor.

'Close the door, please, dear,' the old lady asked Gracie. Then she picked up an envelope that was lying next to her pillow. 'Then please promise me, Doctor, that you will take this to my lawyer, whose address you know. I have written out my instructions, and when you have witnessed the signature, Gracie will also sign it across the seal. I would rather not trust it to the post.'

A flash of cold shock struck Gracie. Did the old lady feel her death was near? She seemed so much brighter than she had been yesterday, almost as if she had rallied. But sometimes people did that just before they died. Why should Gracie care so much? She knew the answer to that: because the old lady trusted her.

The door was closed. The doctor was waiting.

The old lady took a folded piece of paper from the envelope, opened it, and read it over, as if making certain it was what she wished. Then she looked up at the doctor. 'Have you a pen with you, Dr Bramwell?'

Wordlessly, he felt inside his jacket pocket and brought out a fountain pen. He took off the cap and passed the pen to her.

'Thank you,' she said gravely. She signed the bottom of the sheet slowly and carefully.

'Can you read?' the doctor asked Gracie. It clearly made him uncomfortable to place her in such an embarrassing situation. 'Or at least make a mark, and—'

'I can write,' Gracie said a little stiffly. 'And I certainly can read.'

'Can you!' He clearly looked taken aback, then he glanced at the old lady in some confusion.

'Get her to sign it on the back of the envelope, when it's sealed,' she instructed patiently.

The doctor did that. First, his own signature on the open page. Then, he folded it and put it back into the envelope and, following Gracie's signing the outside of it, he addressed it to the solicitor. 'I will put this in their letter box as I pass it tonight,' he promised. 'It will be there for them in the morning.'

The old lady looked at him steadily for a moment, then seemed satisfied. With a nod, she said, 'Thank you.'

The doctor spent a moment or two more, listening to his patient's heart, pressing his fingers into her wrist. 'Seems quite fine,' he said, looking at her gravely. Then he turned to Gracie. 'I'll come again quite soon.' He gave a brief smile and shifted his attention back to the old lady. 'I am delighted to see you looking so much more comfortable. Happy Christmas.'

'Thank you,' she answered. 'And to you, too. Let us hope you do not get called out!'

Gracie saw the doctor down the stairs and met Julia Harcourt standing in the hall. It was evident to Gracie that she was waiting for them.

'Thank you, you can go,' she said to Gracie, then turned to the doctor.

Gracie stepped back obediently, but stopped just behind the door in the morning room, where she could still see the hallway. If she made no sound at all, she could hear Julia Harcourt's voice.

'How is she, Doctor? And please, tell me the truth. No comforting and meaningless reassurances.'

The doctor's voice also was quite clear. 'I'm surprised with how much better she looks, and pleased, of course. But I must warn you, Mrs Harcourt, it is only a matter of time, and not a great deal of it, I believe. Just keep her as comfortable as you can.'

'Of course,' she replied. 'And thank you so much for coming, Doctor. It is very reassuring to have your word that we are doing all we can for her.'

Gracie waited to hear his response, but he had hesitated, as if trying to find the right words to say what was on his mind.

'Is there something more we can do?' the woman asked, interrupting the silence.

'I don't think so, no. Mrs Harcourt, I can't …' The doctor did not finish his train of thought.

Gracie imagined a bleak smile, a man who could never say what he knew, especially to a woman who would find his knowledge dangerous. How much did he know? She heard them bid one another goodbye, and the front door opening and closing.

Gracie moved away from the door, just in case Mrs Harcourt should put her head into the room, seeing the door open.

She heard heavy footsteps. Mr Harcourt?

'Well?' his voice demanded. 'What did he say?'

'Soon,' his wife replied. 'He's sure it will not be long. It can't be. Should we—' She stopped. Was she afraid to put the rest of the thought into words?

'Is there anyone we should inform?' he asked levelly, ignoring the question. 'So it will not come as a surprise. We don't want anybody to think ...'

'Stop fussing, Gilbert!' she snapped. 'He told us to expect it, and quite soon. Then we can deal with everything else. We can let at least one of the maids go. Not that it will help much. They don't eat a lot, and the rooms are there anyway. Just don't panic!'

'It will be hard,' he said. There was surprise and regret in his voice.

'Of course, it will be a grief to us, to both of us,' she said more softly. 'I know that. We'll want to take a little time for mourning, and wear black appropriately. Then, we will be ... free.'

He started to speak, then changed his mind.

Gracie heard footsteps going away, across the hall to the stairs. She breathed out a sigh of relief. She was so tense her body ached. In another few minutes, she could return to the servants' quarters and find something to keep herself busy until it was time to telephone Samuel again.

She realised how much she missed him, even to say things that did not matter. It was the sharing that counted. Such as telling him about her day, so he could hear what the children had said and done.

She remembered how he had expected a son, but when Charlie had been born, he had suddenly realised how much he loved her. At first, he had been half afraid to touch her, she was so tiny, so perfect in every detail, and noisy! Demanding. She was screaming the first time he had picked her up. That was all she wanted, attention. She stopped crying and lay quietly in his arms, her tear-stained little face smiling at him. From that moment forward, he was enchanted.

Of course, he came back to reality and learned the need for constant attention. But when she could talk, the bond was really sealed. His patience was as endless as her questions. Perhaps there was nothing Samuel could ever do, and for which Gracie loved him more deeply, more than the patience he gave to his daughter. She could imagine them now, as Charlie told him how to do everything she had seen Gracie do in the kitchen. He knew how to do it as well, but he would listen anyway. He never contradicted her when she told Gracie proudly, 'I teached Daddy!'

This evening, because both Mr and Mrs Harcourt were in the withdrawing room right up to the time they went to bed, Gracie was late calling home.

'Hello, Samuel?' she said breathlessly, when at last she heard him answer.

'Gracie? Are you all right?' There was anxiety in his voice. If he had tried to hide it, he had failed. 'Are you all right?' he repeated.

'Yes. But Mr and Mrs Harcourt are upset and they didn't go to bed until just now.' She did not bother to explain. 'Are you all right? Is everybody well?'

'Yes,' he answered. 'And full of Christmas excitement.'

'Is Charlie bossing you around? Are Tommy and Vic all right?'

'The boys miss you.' He sounded surprised. 'Even more than Charlie does, I think. But not more than I do.'

There was a gentleness in his voice that was almost like being wrapped in a hug. She could feel the warmth filling her. She swallowed hard. 'They're still very little. Even Tommy is only four. But anyway, I keep telling you, little girls are tougher!'

'I don't believe you,' he replied. 'She's just determined not to show it! But she misses you. I've never met such a bossy little piece.' His voice was thick with emotion as he said it.

'She's looking after you.' She had to stop there,

because she could feel tears coming. She could have put the telephone down and returned home tonight. But if she walked out on these people now, though Samuel would understand, Charlie wouldn't. 'I'll be home for Christmas. And don't worry, I'm fine. Good night.'

She hung up the receiver, sniffed hard, and went upstairs.

Gracie slept well that night, but Bessie's knock on the door woke her with a feeling of alarm. She sat up, heart beating hard. It was cold, but for a moment she was unaware of it.

'Cup of tea?' The girl carried the cup balanced carefully, not to spill any of it into the saucer.

'Thank you.' Gracie took it carefully and sipped it. The tea was hot, soothing to the taste.

Bessie hesitated. Plainly, she wanted to say something more.

'What is it?' Gracie asked, putting the cup down.

'You got to look after the old lady, proper, like. Least, as long as you're here.' Her face looked bleak, even frightened.

Gracie understood, even though she had never been in that position. Charlotte Pitt was the only person she had ever worked for, and she had been safe there, always warm enough, well fed and even included in great adventures. But she knew it was not like that for everyone.

Bessie went downstairs again. Gracie got out of bed and dressed as quickly as she could, washed her face and brushed her hair, pinning it back neatly. Then she hurried downstairs to get breakfast before it was cleared away.

All the servants were there, eating quickly and quietly. She said, 'Good morning,' then helped herself to porridge. Cook was good at many things, but her porridge was the one dish Gracie would still miss when she went home. There was even 'top of the bottle', the creamiest part of the milk, to put with it. And brown sugar, if she wanted it. Gracie preferred her porridge plain.

'I'll take some up to the old lady,' she said, rising from her seat and walking over to the side table where the tureen of porridge was set. The tray was prepared and ready to take up. All she needed to do was make the tea and a couple of thin slices of toast. The butter dish and the fresh marmalade were already there.

Ten minutes later, she was upstairs and outside the old lady's room. She set the tray on the side table near the door and knocked lightly. It was a small courtesy, perhaps, but she felt it necessary.

There was no answer.

She knocked again, a little more loudly.

Still no answer.

She turned the handle and went in. The curtains were open and the room was full of sunlight. The old lady was still lying down, a slight smile on her face, as if she were expecting someone would be coming whom she liked, someone who would be kind to her, and gentle.

Gracie walked over silently and touched her on the arm. It was cold. Gracie touched her cheek very softly. It also was cold, and she did not stir.

Gracie felt a wave of grief so sharp that tears prickled in her eyes. It was not a tragedy; it was the quiet end of life. And it had clearly been peaceful, yet Gracie was still overcome by loss. It was a while before she moved. She thought there must be some custom dictating that she close the curtains. But why? The sunlight seemed natural, especially now.

She walked back to the door, leaving the tray. Someone could get it later. She went down the stairs and to the butler's pantry. The door was closed. She knocked.

Mr Denning answered. He saw her expression. 'What's wrong, Gracie?' There was alarm in his face.

'Nothing, Mr Denning. At least …'

He looked at her closely. 'You've been crying! What's happened?'

'I took old Mrs Harcourt's breakfast up to her. She's … she's dead, sir. Lying there smiling in the sun. I've never seen anyone so …' she gulped, 'so much at peace.'

He took a very deep breath and let it out in a sigh. 'Oh, the poor soul. I'm sorry you had to find her. Will you be all right?' He frowned anxiously, clearly concerned for her.

'Oh, yes, thank you,' she replied. 'I'm just upset, because … well, I liked her. I would have liked to have had the chance to be …' She had been about to say 'kind to her', but that implied that the others had not.

He smiled.

'I could have brought her treats and the like,' she added. 'And I wouldn't have cared if they threw me out in the street, except that the Harcourts might be even worse to all of you.'

'Sit down for a few minutes,' he said gently. 'Sit here, if you like. In fact, I think it would be better here. I don't want to upset everybody else, not just yet. I'll go up and see for myself. Then I had better inform the master and mistress.'

'Do you want me to come with you, seeing as I was the one who found her?' She wanted to go, partly to support Denning, but also to see what the Harcourts' reaction would be, hearing the news that should have been grief to them, but also brought relief to their urgent financial problems. She had forgotten the snatch of conversation she had overheard in the hall. Of course, she had not read the note that the doctor had signed and taken, but now she wondered what it was. She waited for the butler to reply.

'If you don't find it too distressing, perhaps it would be a good idea,' he said, after a few moments. 'I will come back for you, if you wait here. Please do not speak to any of the others just yet. We need to inform them properly, after I have seen the Harcourts.'

'Yes, sir.'

When he came back for her, they went together to the dining room, where the Harcourts were just beginning breakfast. For a moment or two, they ignored Denning.

'Excuse me, sir.'

'What is it?' Mr Harcourt asked abruptly. 'Can't it wait until we have finished eating, for heaven's sake?'

'I don't think so, sir,' Denning replied.

Harcourt must have caught something in the tone of Denning's voice, because he placed his fork on his plate and turned to look at the man. 'Well, what is it?'

'I'm sorry to tell you, sir, but your mother passed away during the night.'

'What did you say?' Harcourt looked startled.

'It seems to have been very peaceful, sir.'

'How do you know? And –' he gestured towards Gracie, '– what's this damn maid doing here? This is a family matter!'

'Gracie was the one who found her, sir. She was taking up breakfast.'

Harcourt swivelled in his chair to look at Gracie. 'That's not your job,' he began. Then perhaps realising the absurdity of the remark, and under these circumstances, he stopped abruptly. 'Peacefully?' he asked Gracie. 'How do you know?'

'Because she was lying in the sun and smiling,' Gracie answered. The old lady had been at peace, feeling safe, clean and with dignity. She did not say all this, though, because she did not wish to comfort Harcourt.

'Perhaps she was just asleep.' Mrs Harcourt spoke for the first time. 'You made a mistake. We must send someone less hysterical.'

'She is not hysterical, ma'am,' Denning said, possibly more sharply than he intended. There was very little respect in his tone. 'I went up myself, before informing you. Mrs Harcourt must have died sometime during the night, quite early.'

'How do you know that?' Mrs Harcourt demanded.

Denning winced slightly. 'Because she was cold to the touch, ma'am,' he replied. 'I would not have informed you without making sure myself. Do you wish me to send for the doctor?'

'What on earth can he do?' She glared at Denning.

'He needs to sign the death certificate, ma'am,' he replied. 'I'm sure you would like everything to be legally correct.' If he meant anything more than the mere words, it was not reflected in his face.

Gracie wondered if he knew, or guessed, how desperately the Harcourts had been waiting for this.

'Yes,' Mr Harcourt said. 'Yes, of course. We must inform the doctor. And the lawyers. And I suppose there will be letters to write. Family living at a distance, and so on.'

'Yes, sir. Would you like to make the funeral arrangements yourself, or may I be of assistance?' Denning offered.

Harcourt looked momentarily confused. Gracie thought that surely this eventuality could not have caught him off-guard. He must have been expecting it, and soon. He had been perfectly aware of it, since he had discussed it with his wife when they thought themselves alone.

'Thank you, Denning, that would be most helpful of you. And please inform the rest of the servants. They have to know, but ... but try not to let them get out of hand. She was an old lady. It is the natural and peaceful end to a long life.'

'Yes, sir,' Denning said obediently. He turned to Gracie. 'We must leave Mr and Mrs Harcourt to come to terms with their grief. We need to take care of a considerable number of things.'

'Not Gracie,' Mrs Harcourt said sharply. 'Ask the others. I don't know her and—'

Denning interrupted her, which Gracie suspected was something he had never done before. 'Ma'am, all the staff are going to be distressed. Many of them have not encountered death before, not of someone they knew. Gracie was kind to her, but a week ago she had never heard of her, and she can read and write, which will be useful to me just now.' His voice sounded more like delivering an instruction than offering a plea.

Mr Harcourt nodded briefly. 'Just take care of it, Denning. Oh, and you'd better telephone the doctor now.'

'Yes, sir, of course.' Denning gave Gracie a quick glance, and then left the room.

She followed immediately on his heels. When she caught up with him, he looked very pale. He must have been expecting the old lady to die, and yet he seemed shocked. 'Are you all right, Mr Denning?' she asked him anxiously.

He looked startled, and then coloured faintly pink. 'Yes. Yes, thank you. It's only that one death reminds you of others, maybe from long ago. There's something the same about all of them. Makes you think of mortality, the end of things. As you get older … you know.' He turned away and began walking along the corridor again.

She hurried to keep up with him. 'Mr Denning.'

'Yes?'

'She made an addition to her will yesterday afternoon. I didn't read it, just signed my name to say that I'd seen her sign it. And on the back of the envelope. A witness. The doctor said he would deliver it to the lawyer, but you'd better make sure he did.'

Denning stopped. 'Yesterday afternoon? You saw it?'

'Yes, sir. I signed right over where it was sealed.'

'Clever,' he said. 'Clever girl. When I call the lawyer, I will make sure he got that envelope. Thank you, Gracie. You helped make the old lady's last day or two a lot better.'

'Remember, she was lying there in the morning sunlight, smiling,' she said quietly. 'You may want to tell the others that.'

'I will. I will.'

It was late morning when the doctor came. Julia Harcourt insisted on taking him upstairs herself. Gracie heard only a snatch of their conversation.

'I didn't expect it to be so soon,' the doctor said, going across the landing, his feet almost silent on the carpet. 'I'm so sorry.'

'It's not … questionable … is it?' she asked.

'Oh, no, my dear, it's quite normal. She could have

gone any time. At least she was not in pain or distress. It was probably in her sleep.'

'You have to see her. Then you can sign the certificate.' She said this as if she needed to be assured. From Gracie's view, it sounded a little like a question.

'Yes, of course. This is a natural death. An easy way to go, if you can say such a thing. Of course, you will miss her.'

That was preposterous! In the several days that Gracie had been in the house, Mrs Harcourt had never gone anywhere near the old lady. And she certainly had offered her no companionship and no comfort. Mr Harcourt had been up once, that Gracie knew of, and had taken a cup of tea with her only when Gracie had suggested it. The only ones who sat with her, spoke to her as a person, not just part of the job, were the youngest servants: Mary, Bessie, and perhaps Millie, when she was here. Who was Mrs Harcourt hoping to impress? Would the doctor believe her? Or was the doctor a party to their lies?

The doctor and Mrs Harcourt walked past the storeroom where Gracie was standing, just behind the door and pretending to sort through cushions and extra cushion covers. As they went towards the next flight of stairs, she lost their voices.

She stepped out of the door and went downstairs. Miss Allsop was standing just outside the kitchen door, a flatiron in her hand. She looked pale.

'Sit down, Miss Allsop,' Cook encouraged her. 'You'll miss the old lady. We all will, but she's better off where she's gone. Do you want a cup of tea? Got some more cake here. Madeira. Made it yesterday.'

'Yes, I think I will. Thank you, Mrs Bland,' Allsop replied, putting the iron down on the table. 'I suppose the next thing will be to get out everything black that the young Mrs Harcourt has. I wonder how long she'll pretend to be mourning? Odd, wearing black for Christmas. She will miss a few fancy parties, I suppose. Best that I put away the red dress.' A small smile curled her lips. 'Perhaps she will feel she cannot go at all, and that will put her in a foul mood!'

She became aware of Gracie behind her. 'Little pigs with long ears!' she said tartly, and then picked up the flatiron. 'Go and put this away, before somebody drops it.'

'Yes, Miss Allsop,' Gracie said obediently, taking the iron. 'I suppose they're putting wreaths on the front door?'

'Holly and ivy, with berries?' Miss Allsop said with a frown. 'I doubt it. It's hardly fitting!'

'No, Miss Allsop, I meant a funeral type of wreath,' Gracie corrected her. 'I'd like that, if they did. If they don't, we could put up one ourselves, on the back door.'

Miss Allsop drew in her breath sharply, then slowly her eyes widened. 'What an excellent idea! You are useful for something after all. We can put out a formal one, a big one, with white flowers in it, like we lost someone special.'

'That's a good idea,' Cook agreed. 'And we can draw our curtains half over, the way they do for a family member.'

'She was a family member,' Gracie responded. 'It doesn't get any closer than your own mother!'

Cook stared at her. 'They are … quality, so they're different from us.'

'No, they aren't,' Gracie snapped back at her, remembering all the emotions she had seen, and having been so close to, when she had lived and worked with the Pitts. 'There are decent folk everywhere, who work night and day to find the truth, to help people like themselves, and people like us, or anyone. There are good people and bad everywhere. I worked for a top policeman, and I saw him risk his own life to save the Queen, and also to get justice for the lowest there is, off the backstreets of Whitechapel. And I won't stand by while you say different!' She stopped abruptly. What she had said frightened her, because it was stupid to have said it. It was true, it was one of the truest things she had said, but it would prevent her from … what? Finding out the truth of what had happened to the old lady? If there was any truth to find.

'I'm sorry, Mrs Bland,' she said quietly. 'I shouldn't have said that. It's true, mind you, but it's out of place now. What we need to know is whether the old lady was treated right last night. And we need to stop Mrs Harcourt from throwing anyone out … at Christmas!' She stared defiantly at Cook, her face announcing that she was not going to budge an inch on that.

To her surprise, Cook was startled, even thoughtful, rather than furious at Gracie's impertinence. 'What can we do?' she asked slowly, framing each word as if even by themselves each one had meaning.

'I don't know,' Gracie admitted. 'I have to think.'

Should she tell Cook what she had overheard from the dressing room? She looked at the older woman's face, flushed with the heat of the stove, where she had been working, making sauce in a pan, now finished. But the woman's hair straggled out of the white cap she wore to keep it tidy, and her face was creased with worry. This was her home. Her job. The young Mrs Harcourt was never going to come into the kitchen to cook a meal! Gracie guessed that she didn't know how to boil an egg, never mind braise fish, cook a roast right through without burning the outside, or even think about baking a cake or a loaf of bread. And she was far too vain and careful of her appearance to let go of a creative lady's maid like Allsop. She probably could not sew a button on straight, let alone design and stitch a new gown. But she would be sure that someone would be dismissed, even if only to show what could happen to any of them, and that she was in charge. It might even be Mr Denning, and that would be terrible. He might find another place quite easily, if given a good reference. But this was more than his home; this was his family, all the family he had.

But maybe the old lady had a little money of her own. Mr and Mrs Harcourt had spoken as if she had, and that it would now come to them. Was that at the core of it, what it was all about?

'We have to be careful,' Gracie continued, but we

also must remember that they don't have all the power.'

'Yes, they do!' Cook contradicted.

'No, they don't,' Gracie said firmly. 'There are ten of us. We have courage and we have brains. If we stick together, and no one turns on the rest of us, there must be something we can do.'

Cook shook her head, but it was puzzlement, not denial. 'I don't know whether you're brave or daft. But I don't see as we have any choice left.'

'Well, they can't do anything to me.' Even as she said the words, Gracie hoped they were true.

'I suppose they won't do anything this side of Christmas. It would look awful,' Cook said with new hope in her face, as if she were beginning to see the possibilities.

The following day, Mrs Jenkins came to Gracie, almost as soon as breakfast was finished. She did not speak to her in the servants' dining room, but asked Gracie to come with her to the housekeeper's sitting room, which was private.

'Yes, ma'am?' Gracie said nervously. She was afraid this was going to be a dismissal, probably at Julia Harcourt's insistence. She stood in front of Mrs

Jenkins as if expecting a blow, yet with her head high and her eyes squarely meeting those of the housekeeper. Mrs Jenkins looked tired, her eyes larger than usual in her thin, sensitive face. How many times had she had to do this?

'Gracie, I'm sorry to ask you, but it is necessary, and I believe you will do it with honesty and respect. It is too much to ask of the younger girls.'

Gracie could not think of anything to say.

Mrs Jenkins drew in her breath. She looked far older than she must actually have been. There were fine lines about her eyes and mouth, and a tiny muscle flickered in her temple. 'I want you to clean out the old lady's room,' she said quietly. 'The undertakers took her body late yesterday evening. You need to be as discreet as possible, not to distress those of us who cared for her. I don't feel I can ask Mary and Bessie to do this.' She took a faltering breath. 'We must clean out all her clothes, wash any if necessary, although I doubt there will be much. But keep her things.' She stopped, looking carefully at Gracie, as if to see if she had grasped what she could not bring herself to say.

Gracie cleared her throat. 'Do you mean,' she asked softly, and a bit awkwardly, 'to see that nothing goes missing? For the protection of someone who might want a keepsake?' This was a very roundabout way of asking if it was to protect any of the younger staff from a charge of theft.

'Yes, that is what I mean,' Mrs Jenkins replied. 'And see that nothing is unaccounted for, that anyone might be blamed.'

'Miss Allsop?' Gracie said inadvertently. 'The old lady had some beautiful things that Allsop admired, so it would be natural if … if the old lady had promised her … something.' She did not allow herself to finish the thought.

'I mean by anyone at all,' Mrs Jenkins snapped. 'Including Mrs Harcourt herself. Whatever the will says, we must wait until it is read before we decide that we cannot find various things. Things she may have wished to go to one friend or another.' She stopped, her face pink, her eyes suddenly filling with tears. She wanted to appear strict, but it was a protective disguise, too easy for the emotions to break through.

Gracie found herself hoping intensely that the old lady had left Mrs Jenkins something, a lace handkerchief or a pin, or a scarf to remember her by.

'Yes, Mrs Jenkins,' she replied with a nod. 'I'll

be careful to include everything, and I won't let anyone take anything, in case the old lady might have made a bequest to someone. That would be thieving – begging your pardon for using such a word.'

'Quite correct, Gracie, it is the right word. We mustn't allow it. It is the one last thing we can do, now that it's too late to do anything else.' There was sharp regret, perhaps even guilt, in her face. And a deep sorrow.

The winter sun filled the room again today, and although the old lady's body had been taken away, Gracie still felt her presence. Thoughts filled her mind as to where her spirit might be. What did she really believe about death, and a life afterwards? What she said about this to anyone was what she had been taught, but was it really so?

The day before yesterday the old lady had been so much here, and now there were only her belongings, and they were not really her. Her family would divide up the spoils, like animals feeding on the dead.

*Don't be disgusting!* she told herself sharply. That inner voice reminded her that the old lady had meant people to have her things. Now she needed to get them sorted, carefully, each thing where anyone would see it. Clothes in piles, books, ornaments, everything where it could be seen. Take the dust off! Make them look cared for! Give her some dignity. These had been her treasures, only two days ago.

The bed had already been stripped and the linen taken down to the laundry. Gracie thought she should take the quilt back to her own room. She had been cold without it, but glad that she had lent it to the old lady.

She began with the clothes in the wardrobe. There were not many of them, but they were very good quality and someone had cared for them. Nothing seemed to need mending. Blouses had been ironed and hung up carefully. Gracie took them out one by one, separating them from the coat hangers they had been put on so they would not be creased. They weren't crumpled in the least. They had been hung up with care, as if they might be worn again. They were all delicate colours. Not bright reds or blues, which would have made the old lady look washed out, even older than she was. But whites and creams, pale pinks, soft grey-blues and lilacs, which would have been lovely on her.

How long had it been since she had worn these

silks and laces, chiffons, and this light-as-a-feather wool? One blouse in deep cream, with heavy lace at the neck and cuffs, was the most beautiful that Gracie had ever seen.

There was a dark blouse, black silk, so fine Gracie could see the pale skin of her own hand through the sleeves. It was plain, yet suitable for the most fashionable dinner, at the Palace even! Or for mourning, to make everyone think a beautiful thing was lost, but maybe not irretrievably.

Her mind was wandering. She must stop it!

There were dresses as well. And shoes sat on a rack set to one side of the wardrobe. She found the smartest pair of black leather boots that laced, criss-crossing up the front.

She brought out another dress, and then two more. They were a little old-fashioned, if one followed the changes year by year. But they were beautiful. One was of wool, for winter wear. It had many seams in it, so it would keep its shape. It was a soft lavender grey, with a swishing skirt that would have swayed just a little when she walked. How elegant! How feminine. Where had she worn it? Was it so very long ago? There was nothing dated about it.

The other dress was a shade between blue and

green, very delicate. Then there was yet another, and another still, all of various colours, all muted. It made Gracie think of a flower garden in the wind!

So many hats! A really beautiful woman had to have hats! Big hats with wide brims and flowers on them. She had to get a chair to stand on, in order to see the very top shelf in the wardrobe. Had the old lady been obliged to ask someone tall, perhaps Allsop or Mrs Jenkins, to get them down for her?

Gracie had to reach up, very precariously, to pull out the hats one by one, and carry them gently to the bed. There was a pink one, decorated with deeper pink roses; a cream one with an even wider brim, decorated with cream roses with golden stamens in the centre. And, of course, a black one with veils and more roses. Every lady had to have a black hat, with a veil.

She took the rest of the dresses, more ordinary ones for every day, and put them all on the bed. She could not bear to think of the present Mrs Harcourt wearing them. Was it disgustingly childish to hope it was impossible for Allsop to alter them to fit the shorter, wider woman?

Stop daydreaming and get on with it! Allsop could probably do almost anything with clothes. It was a pity she didn't have someone more elegant to work with.

Gracie came to the drawers in which monogrammed, lace-edged handkerchiefs were neatly folded. Gracie was certain there would be keepsakes there for those who had cared about the old lady. They would make excellent gifts.

Next, she came to the scarves. There were several of them, wool for winter, finely woven and in cheerful patterns and colours. The ones that caught Gracie's eye were the silk scarves, two in particular. The first one was in brilliant shades of red: crimson, scarlet, vermillion and cerise. There were golden splashes of roses with softer, duller leaves, more like shadows behind the glory of the flowers. The silk slipped through her fingers like liquid. The other scarf was in blues and greens, tropical seas with the light on them, the colours of water in the sun. Or in the imagination.

Gracie was standing in the sunlight streaming through the windows when she was jerked back into the present by footsteps in the passage outside. 'Come in?' she answered to the knock on the door.

Bessie came in slowly. 'You all right?'

'Yes, thank you.'

'Do you want some lunch? It's cold mutton and hot bubble and squeak.' Bessie smiled, as if pleased at the thought.

'Oh, yes!' Gracie said with feeling. She loved bubble and squeak. Yesterday's mashed potatoes chopped up with cabbage and onions, and fried together. It was good with almost anything, but especially cold meat, the way Cook did it. Actually, Gracie was pretty good at it, too. She knew to fry the onions separately, and then put them with the rest afterwards, and serve it hot. 'Yes,' she said again. She put the silk scarves down and went to the door, closing it softly and following Bessie along the passageway.

It was a delicious but sombre meal. Everyone was grieving for the old lady, and for themselves, because they were reminded of other people they had loved, and who had died before them, who had left behind precious times, lives they had been part of. They spoke softly to each other. The younger girls looked a little tear-stained and sniffy. Archie suddenly seemed very adult, steady and comforting. He gave Gracie a swift smile, then looked at Mary again. He was caring for others, perhaps without realising that this was the best way of all to find comfort for himself.

When Allsop got up a few minutes before Gracie had finished her pudding, she put down her spoon and went after the woman. She caught up with her a dozen yards away, just outside the laundry room door. 'Miss Allsop.'

Allsop turned round, her eyebrows raised. 'Yes? What is it?'

Gracie had not rehearsed in her mind what she meant to say, but Allsop's thin, dark face required an immediate answer. 'I've been cleaning and tidying the old lady's room all morning.'

'I know. I could have done that myself!' She sounded angry.

'I was told to.'

'I know that, too. What is it, Gracie?' she asked, impatience in her voice.

'There are a lot of things that are precious, but might get lost because … well, Mrs Harcourt wouldn't know what to do with them.'

'And do you want them?' Allsop's black eyebrows rose in a bitter expression.

Gracie kept her temper with difficulty. Allsop was grieving, as they all were, and perhaps the mere facts of age and death were forceful reminders of what they had seen in the past, of people they may have loved, and of what lay ahead for all of them some day.

'No,' she said. 'But there are things like lace on the edge of a petticoat that is still good, although the fabric's worn. A good seamstress could take it off and use it on something else. It isn't difficult. I could do it myself, but you have the right to. It's wicked to waste lace that is still perfect, just because it's stitched to a piece of cloth that's worn through.'

Allsop's face softened. 'Yes, it is,' she agreed. 'Did you do that once? I mean, as a lady's maid?'

'I was the only maid for Mrs Pitt before I got married, and before she became Lady Pitt. I did all sorts of things. Not like you. I couldn't have made a dress from an idea in my head. But I could sew and mend, reuse things, make them longer or shorter. Make a little girl's dress out of a lady's dress. She didn't have much money then, but her sister was rich. Didn't want for anything.'

'Do you have any little girls?' Allsop asked, her voice softer.

'Yes, Charlie. She's five, going on six. And two boys, younger.' Ridiculously, she found her throat tightening, as if she were going to cry. What was she doing in this miserable house, leaving them alone just before Christmas? Did they know she was coming back soon, really know it? Had Samuel told them again, and again?

Allsop looked puzzled. 'Charlie?'

'It's Charlotte, but we call her Charlie. I don't like Lottie. It's not anything like her namesake Charlotte, Mrs Pitt. Lady Pitt.'

'You called her after Lady Pitt?' Allsop asked.

'Yes, I did. We did.'

Allsop's face softened. 'That's nice.'

'And the boy's after Sir Thomas. We call him Tommy.'

'And the other one?'

'He's Vic – Victor.'

'Who's that after?'

'Lord Narraway. He was Victor.'

'A special friend?'

'Yes, he married Lady Vespasia, but we couldn't call anyone after her because …'

'Her name is too unusual,' said Allsop, supplying the answer.

'Yes, and another reason. There wasn't anybody else who was like her, and there never will be.'

'I see.' Allsop smiled and her eyes looked far into the distance.

Gracie sensed that she was imagining Lady Vespasia, but she knew this couldn't be done. Anyone who had not known Lady Vespasia could not even imagine her. But it would be rude to say so, and perhaps hurtful. Better to change the subject.

'There are things in the drawers and closets that should be treated with care. Beautiful things,' she went on. 'Full of memories of when old Mrs Harcourt was younger. They could be altered a bit, maybe, for someone to use.'

Allsop's eyebrows rose again. 'Someone like Mrs Harcourt?'

'No!' Gracie rejected the thought instantly. Mrs Harcourt had no respect for the old lady.

Allsop stared at Gracie, her face filled with conflicting emotions, all of them painful. 'Why not?' Her voice was little more than a whisper.

What would they do to Gracie if she spoke the truth? Throw her out? They would do that anyway, as soon as they did not need her. 'Because they should go to someone who cares, and they don't,' she said. 'They ignored her to death!'

'Don't say that again, Gracie,' Allsop warned, her voice hard with anxiety.

'It's true!'

'I know it's true,' she agreed, white-faced. 'But you mustn't say it. They'll try to hurt you.'

'I'm going anyway.'

Allsop put her hands up, as if to shake Gracie by the shoulders. 'Listen to me!' Then she realised what she was doing and let them fall to her sides. 'You don't want to have the police come after you, because they say some of the silver is missing! Or worse, a piece of the old lady's jewellery.'

Gracie gasped, a quickly withdrawn breath on which she nearly choked. That would be horribly embarrassing for Samuel! He would be furious. He would know that she had not done anything of the sort, but would everybody else know that? He would be humiliated.

Allsop must have seen her horror. 'I know,' she said, her voice surprisingly gentle. 'You never stole a thing in your life. But that won't matter if someone like Mrs Harcourt says you did. They've got all the power, and they know it.'

'Not all of it,' Gracie said, swallowing back tears of rage, as well as fear and frustration. She lifted her chin a little. 'Then we have to be careful. I don't care if you sack me when I finish clearing that room. In fact—'

'I'll come up and help you finish it,' Allsop told her, making it a statement rather than an offer. 'I'll get the lace. And we can speak for each other.'

'Thank you.'

'Safety,' Allsop explained.

It took them the rest of the afternoon to go through everything, primarily because they did it very carefully.

Allsop examined the lace. 'It is perfect,' she agreed approvingly. 'Some of it is good enough to put on the collar of a blouse. It's wrong to throw it away. Took some poor soul days to make that.'

Gracie refused to think of the needlework, and the strain on the eyes of someone working by candlelight to loop the fine threads, hour after hour. She had never owned lace herself, and was torn as to whether she wanted to. But if no one bought it, what happened to the lace makers then?

They worked in silence most of the time, but an occasional glance at Allsop's face revealed to Gracie most of her feelings. She did not comment. Perhaps that was because it was necessary to keep things private, and better left that way. Out in the open, they might hurt too much.

170

Allsop looked at the dresses, her hands caressing the fabric, letting it fall almost like liquid from her fingers. Once she caught Gracie looking at her. 'Mrs Harcourt won't wear them,' she said, as if answering a question. She saw Gracie's expression. 'She wouldn't fit into them, and there isn't enough fabric in the seams to let out.'

'Good.' Gracie found herself smiling.

They collected the pictures off the walls. They were mostly landscapes, one of them a seascape, all blues and greys of stormy water, and yet they were amazingly restful, perhaps because there was nothing man-made in them, just nature.

They also collected the silver-backed brush and hand mirror, and a small round crystal vase with a silver top, all with a matching pattern.

'What's that for?' Gracie asked, handling it gently.

'Putting things in,' Allsop replied. 'I suppose it could be anything from a regularly worn pair of earrings to safety pins, or spare buttons.'

They sorted the jewellery together. There were not many pieces. They went through them one at a time, each tagged in Allsop's careful handwriting, along with a brief description of it.

'I expect they were all gifts,' Allsop said quietly. 'From someone who loved her.'

'I hope …' Gracie started, and then did not know what she hoped that she could say aloud.

They worked on quietly, and at last came to the papers and books. There were not many of them. Some old letters caused Gracie and Allsop considerable anxiety.

Allsop stood in the fading light; at this time of the year, it was dark shortly after four o'clock. 'Who could we give these to?' she asked, holding up the letters. Her face was creased with confusion.

Gracie knew exactly what she meant. They had no right to destroy them, and yet they might be private. Now was the moment when they must either give them to somebody they trusted – and that was not either of the Harcourts – or put them beyond anybody's reach.

Gracie stared at Allsop and saw the conflict and the pity in her face. 'Perhaps we should give them to Mr Denning?' she suggested. 'Or will he feel obliged to give them to Mrs Harcourt?'

Allsop remained silent for several moments before she made up her mind. 'I'll wrap them up in something that doesn't matter, an old scarf, perhaps, and give them to Cook.'

'Cook?' Gracie was puzzled.

Allsop thought about this for a long moment. 'She might mistake them for rubbish and burn them in the cooker. We do put stuff there sometimes. It's very hot, indeed. Just in case there is something private.'

Gracie looked at the woman. Was she saying that they should burn the lot? 'Should we look?' Gracie asked. 'A quick look? To make sure there isn't anything legal. But I don't think there is, because she gave the doctor an addition to her will the last time he was here.'

Allsop was glancing at the letters. They all seemed to be old, already read, and kept for sentiment's sake. 'I think they're private,' she said at last. 'I shall take them downstairs. I don't think anyone else should read them.'

'Love letters?' Gracie asked, and then wished she had not. It was no one else's concern.

'Yes,' Allsop said softly. 'Private.' She said nothing more, but wrapped them in an old winter scarf that Gracie judged no one would miss. A moment later, she was out the door and closing it softly behind her.

Gracie knew that these letters would soon be reduced to ashes. Perhaps they should not have done this, yet she had the deepest feeling that it was the right thing to do for the old lady, who could not have done it herself. Being so frail, she had no means of destroying anything, and would not have trusted anyone else. And she would not have burdened Bessie or Mary with possession of them, let alone the task of burning them.

The last thing she did was to take down the few books from the shelf. There was a Bible and, not surprisingly, a novel by Charles Dickens, which did not look as if it had been read; several by Jane Austen and the Brontë sisters. Sitting by itself was Robert Louis Stevenson's *Treasure Island*. Gracie opened it and found a piece of paper tucked into the first page. *For Archie, may you find adventures of the mind and treasures of the heart. Sincerely, Adelina Harcourt.*

Where could she put it to be sure Archie got it? Not anywhere that either of the Harcourts could find it. The answer was obvious: Mr Denning. It was the last bequest from an old lady who cared what happened to a young boy. It must be delivered.

Gracie woke up the next morning while it was still dark. Someone was knocking on the door. 'Come in,' she called, forcing herself to keep her eyes open.

She put her arm out of the blankets and then pulled it back from the cold air. The extra quilt made a difference.

Bessie came in with a steaming cup of tea. 'You all right?' she asked.

'Yes, I think so.'

Bessie put the cup down, but she did not leave.

'What is it?' Gracie asked, picking up the cup and sipping from it. It was fresh tasting and just the right temperature. She lowered the cup and looked at Bessie.

'It's Christmas tomorrow,' Bessie said.

'Yes, I know.' Gracie gave a bleak half-smile. It did not feel like Christmas at all.

'You going home to your husband and kids?'

Gracie hesitated. More than almost anything else, she wanted to go home. And she had promised her family she would. Samuel would understand if she failed, but the children would not. Especially Charlie. She had promised Charlie she would be home for Christmas. And yet she could not just walk out and leave these people, who faced a cold and frightening Christmas, followed by the threat of being out in the street. There was nobody to fight for them.

But then, there never had been. Only the illusion that the old lady had some kind of influence. She was gone now, and all she had possessed would belong to Mr Harcourt.

Bessie was still waiting.

'I don't know,' Gracie said quietly. 'Maybe for Christmas, then I could come back. But ...'

'But we could all be out by then,' Bessie said through tears.

'I'll look for another place for each of you.' Gracie had no idea whether she could find more than one or two, but there was nothing else to say. A moment too late, she realised that being on the street was not the only thing Bessie was afraid of, possibly not even the worst. It was being separated from those whom she regarded as family. The people who understood her, liked her, taught her how to do her work, and things about the world in general. People who would look after her if she were ill, share jokes with her, generally be all the things that a family should be.

'Don't give up yet,' Gracie said. 'It's Christmas. Anything could happen.' What a daft thing to say! 'I'll be down for breakfast,' she added. 'I'm not going yet.'

*

All the servants were at the breakfast table. It was probably her imagination, but Gracie felt as if they expected something from her. She had no idea what she could do, or even say, that would help. A promise she could not keep would be worse than no promise at all.

Later, it was Nora, the parlour maid, who put it into words. She was alone with Gracie in the ironing part of the laundry room. 'They got away with it,' Nora said bitterly. 'I knew they done it!'

'What?' Gracie had not been paying attention. She was not used to working with three irons, all heated on the kitchen oven top and used until they were too cold to be effective, and then the next one had to be hot enough to get out the creases, but not so hot as to scorch the white linen.

'Ignored her to death, that's what,' Nora said bitterly. 'And we didn't know how to stop it.' She looked down. 'Millie knew that. We tried, but I suppose we're scared, and we don't know how to go against them.'

Gracie knew one immediate answer. She could not acknowledge defeat. But its taste was bitter and certain inside her, and it was just bravado, that was all.

\*

It was late afternoon when Mr Denning himself came to Gracie, where she was counting items in the upstairs linen cupboard. She assumed he was going to instruct her as to when it would be appropriate for her to leave. She felt a void inside herself at the thought. It was not the happiness of homecoming that filled her mind, but rather that feeling of the captain being the first to leave a sinking ship, rather than the last, as was his duty.

'Yes, Mr Denning?' she said, acknowledging his presence, and forcing herself to meet his eyes because it was difficult to do.

'Would you come downstairs, please, Gracie? The lawyer, Mr O'Mara, is here to read the old lady's will, and we are all required to be present.'

'I'm not really staff here,' she began.

'Nevertheless, you are required,' he insisted. 'Whatever you are doing can wait.'

'Yes, sir.' It was a small job, counting linen, filling in time rather than being genuinely useful. She turned and followed him downstairs and into the with-drawing room, where the full household staff was already assembled. Mr and Mrs Harcourt were there, and a man Gracie had not seen before but whom she presumed to be the lawyer. He was younger than she had expected, perhaps not more than in his forties, with a curious, quizzical face, not suitable for reading wills at all. Rather more like that of a man who took up unlikely cases to argue in court.

No one introduced him, or told him who Gracie was. He glanced at her briefly, then seemed to address them all, rather than only the master and mistress, who were presumably the only legally interested parties. He read from a sheaf of papers in his hand.

'*I, Adelina Mary Harcourt, being of sound mind and under no duress, do bequeath everything of which I am possessed in the following manner, unto the said persons.*' He looked around the room and smiled, as if he were the host of a party to which they were all equally guests.

Gracie found her back ached from sitting upright in a chair designed for relaxing into, and her finger-nails were digging into the palms of her hands.

'*Numerous lace-edged and embroidered handker-chiefs to be divided up among the female staff, all to be included equally.*'

'For God's sake,' Mr Harcourt said, not quite under his breath, 'are we going to go through every piece of clothing?'

The lawyer looked up. 'This is the reading of a

will, Mr Harcourt, a very serious matter indeed. We are going to proceed exactly according to the law.' It was clearly a statement, not a request.

Harcourt sat back in his chair, but he was plainly far from pleased. Gracie thought that Mr O'Mara might have been the old lady's lawyer, but he would not remain the Harcourts' lawyer after this.

'*My boots, of which I believe there are five or so pairs, I leave to Mrs Jenkins, the housekeeper. They will fit her, and she spends a lot of time on her feet. She deserves to be well shod.*'

Mrs Harcourt rolled her eyes. She drew in breath to speak, then looked at Mr Harcourt and changed her mind.

Mr O'Mara glanced at her, then bent his eyes to the papers in his hand and continued.

'*To Mrs Bland, the best cook I ever knew, I leave all the cooking equipment in the kitchen, copper pans, steamers, kettles and all the dishes.*'

'This is absurd,' Mrs Harcourt burst out. 'They are not the old lady's to give. Not to the cook or anyone else.'

Gracie glanced at Cook's face and saw the surprise and joy fade from it like sunlight going behind a cloud.

O'Mara looked at Mrs Harcourt. 'It says in the addendum that they were purchased with Adelina Harcourt's money. The receipts are provided. I'm sorry, Mrs Harcourt, but they are hers to leave as she wishes. And what use would they be to you?'

Mrs Harcourt gritted her teeth. 'They belong in my house. If I choose to dismiss Mrs Bland from my service, she does not take anything at all from the kitchen. It would be theft.'

O'Mara smiled. 'You are mistaken, Mrs Harcourt. They now belong to Mrs Bland. If anyone else takes them from this house, unless with her permission, *that* would be theft.'

'For God's sake, Julia, be quiet and let's get this farce over with!' her husband snapped. 'If you are going to argue over every pot and pan, we'll be here all Christmas! It's probably only Mother's way of making sure we don't dismiss the cook. And why would we? We won't find a better one.'

Mrs Harcourt shot him a bitter look, but she said nothing. Gracie thought she probably saw the sense in his argument, but she clearly did not appreciate being contradicted in front of the household staff.

O'Mara looked from one to the other of them.

'Get on with it,' Harcourt ordered. No one else moved.

O'Mara looked to the paper again. '*To Mr Arthur Denning, I leave my books, which I know he loves, mainly those by Jane Austen, Charlotte and Emily Brontë, and any others he may wish for. With the exception of Robert Louis Stevenson's* Treasure Island, *which I leave to Archie Watson, presently employed as boot boy in this house. I know he cannot yet read, but I request that he be taught to do so, and also to write. I suggest Mrs Jenkins might do this. She is well spoken, and has the gift of teaching. It is also my wish that she may teach any other of the younger staff, such as Mary, Bessie and Millie, and even Nora, should she wish it, and that Mrs Jenkins be suitably recompensed for this task.*'

Gracie looked at Archie, sitting bolt upright in a hard-backed chair, his face shining with pure joy.

'And while the housekeeper is playing school-mistress, who is supposed to do her job?' Mrs Harcourt asked sarcastically. 'And Archie is not a great deal of use, but we're not paying him and feeding him and giving him lodging for doing nothing.'

'You are perfectly correct, ma'am,' O'Mara agreed

with a smooth, satisfied smile. 'If I may continue?' He turned and gave Archie, who was now looking worried, a wide smile, then looked back at the papers again. '*To my granddaughter, Marietta Marchment, who presently resides somewhere in the United States of America, I leave my pearl necklace and earrings and my pearl brooch. To my other granddaughter, Eliza Southern, who also lives somewhere in America, I leave my diamond pendant and earrings.*'

Gracie looked at Mrs Harcourt, but her face was unreadable. If she had wanted any of these pieces, the will was perfectly plain.

'*My clothes will not fit my daughter-in-law, but her lady's maid, Evangeline Allsop, is gifted with a needle. In fact, I think she is capable of creating, or recreating, almost anything to wear. She should devote her talent to designing clothes. She will make something useful and beautiful of anything I possess. Therefore, I leave to her all my scarves, lace collars, fichus and other trimmings, except my blue silk scarf and my red silk scarf. These I leave to Gracie Tellman, the blue one for herself and the red one for her daughter, Charlotte Tellman, known as Charlie. And I leave money in the sum of ten pounds for Thomas and Victor as well, with instructions to their father*

*to buy them a mechanical train set, which I believe
they have desired.'*

Now it was Gracie's turn to be stunned. She gasped
in surprise. She had known the old lady only a few
days! She had only spoken of Charlie and the other
children once. Was that why the old lady had asked
the doctor to deliver an addition to the will?

Everyone was staring at her. She felt the heat rise
up her face.

'Very thoughtful,' Denning said quite distinctly.

'Balderdash!' Mrs Harcourt said, finally losing
control of her temper. 'That surely proves she was
out of her mind! Leaving a valuable silk scarf to a
temporary servant and another to her child, for heav-
en's sake!' She looked at Gracie and then back at
O'Mara. 'A week ago, she had never heard of her!'

'A scarf?' the lawyer said. 'It seems quite natural
to me. This … Gracie … was apparently kind to her.
She also left one hundred pounds to you, Mr Harcourt,
and one hundred pounds to Dr Bramwell. Was that
also nonsensical?'

Mr Harcourt thought for a few seconds only, before
making up his mind. 'Yes,' he said. 'It is. Bramwell
was doing no more than his duty, for which he is
paid. And since I am the main heir, an extra one

hundred pounds is superfluous. In fact, it is proof her mind was going.'

'I have not finished, sir,' O'Mara pointed out.

'Then get on with it, man! You are dragging it out like one of the Reverend Thomson's worst sermons.'

O'Mara smiled. He had beautiful teeth. 'Oh, worse than that, I think.' He looked at the paper and continued reading after turning to the next page.

*The four-bedroom country cottage with its garden and all outbuildings, furniture and other conveniences, I leave to my son, Gilbert Harcourt, and my daughter-in-law, Julia Harcourt. It is freehold, and without any alteration or serious redecorating will make an excellent residence.'*

'Of course it will,' Mrs Harcourt said with satisfaction. 'I think we will sell it. We do not need it.'

'No need to,' her husband replied. 'Mother took care of her money very well. There will be more than we need. The cottage is a nice property and it will only appreciate. Thank you, O'Mara. I take it there are no other specific bequests?'

'No, sir,' O'Mara replied, again showing his teeth. 'Except for this house, which is detailed specifically, including all its fittings, furnishings, linen, china, silver, et cetera.'

'Take that as read, man!' Harcourt cut him off with a gesture.

'Yes, sir,' said the lawyer. 'And including the money, trusts, certificates and all other properties …'

The Harcourts looked at each other, barely able to conceal their satisfaction.

'*All of these,*' read O'Mara, '*I leave to the servants as now composed, namely: Mr Arthur Denning, Mrs Mary Bland, Mrs Gwyneth Jenkins, Miss Evangeline Allsop, Mr Robert Walters, Millicent Foster, Nora Jones, Bessie Stubbs, Mary Watson, and Archie Watson.*'

There was utter silence, except for the rasping of breath.

'*It is thus, collectively, for them to live in together,*' O'Mara continued, '*as long as they choose. And the house and its contents may not be sold, except by the will of them all, if they so desire, and that only after the passage of at least ten years from the date of my death. It is my suggestion that they turn it into a small hotel, and run it with their combined skills, so that they may have the income to sustain the property, keep it in good repair, pay out such taxes as are legally required, and have sufficient income to live comfortably, to afford tutelage in reading,*' *writing and basic mathematics to those who may benefit. This is my will and desire. I have included separately varied suggestions on managing the above.'*

O'Mara looked at them all and smiled, adding, 'It is duly signed and witnessed by Adelina Mary Harcourt and dated.'

Mrs Harcourt was the first to recover her voice. 'She was clearly quite mad! She can't do that! Mr O'Mara, this is an absurd joke, and very cruel. You have seriously shocked my husband, and more serious still, you have given these …' She stared around at the stunned servants. 'You have given them ridiculous hopes that cannot possibly be realised.' And then she was at a loss for words. Her face was ashen white.

O'Mara now looked perfectly serious. 'Madam, if it were so, it would indeed have been a cruel and irresponsible practical joke. But I assure you, this is perfectly legal. It is the properly written last will and testament of Adelina Mary Harcourt, made while of sound mind and witnessed by two members of our legal firm. And should you contest the will in any way whatsoever, you will lose title to the cottage, which is in fact a substantial residence. You are not disinherited. Nor are your children. You have a property sufficient to live on, and a small amount of money. There is jewellery for your daughters.'

'This is our home!' Mr Harcourt found words at last, his face drained of all colour.

'It was,' O'Mara corrected him. 'It is now the home of the servants, who apparently were kind to your mother, cared for her. She told me they did this, despite, at times, at risk of being turned out on to the street. I imagine they will not turn you out on Christmas Eve. It would be an uncharitable thing to do, although you do have another property to go to, albeit cold, and without food, as yet. But you have not been disinherited and left with nothing.'

'You can't ...' Mr Harcourt began, his voice high pitched with shock and outrage. Then he looked at O'Mara's face. 'I'll have you disbarred for this!'

'For reading a will?' O'Mara said with disbelief. 'I'd like to see you try.' His face was suddenly very serene. 'You would then end up without even the cottage in the country, Mr Harcourt. All of this is contingent upon your not contesting this will. I don't think your wife would thank you for that. A miserable time of the year to be homeless. Not to mention embarrassing to have to ask your acquaintances to take you in.'

Denning cleared his throat. 'Excuse me, sir.' He was looking at O'Mara. 'I believe my fellow servants would agree with me that Mr and Mrs Harcourt do not need to leave until after Christmas. It would be a cruel time of year to turn anyone on to the streets. They are welcome to stay here tonight, and possibly Christmas night. That will give them time to get to the country property. Although, perhaps another housekeeper will be harder to obtain ...' His voice trailed off.

Julia Harcourt stared first around at the servants, and then at her husband. Her face was ashen, except for two feverish spots of colour on her cheeks. 'Are you going to stand for this?' she shouted incredulously. 'They are robbing us of everything! Everything! Your mother had clearly lost her mind, and you are standing there as if you've lost yours as well!' She swung to face O'Mara. 'And you! It's your job to protect us, and you are ... are ...' She was lost, unable to find the word adequate to describe her contempt.

O'Mara spoke quite clearly. 'No, madam, it is my job to protect the wishes of Mrs Adelina Harcourt, deceased. Her wish was perfectly plain. She desired that this house, and all its furniture of every sort, should belong to the servants, as now constituted. I'm sure I do not need to read out their names again.'

'I don't need to know their names, you fool!' Julia Harcourt snapped. 'My husband is her son. Her only son, I may add. This house, and everything it contains, is rightfully his.'

'No, madam,' O'Mara contradicted her. 'It was Mrs Adelina Harcourt's house. You lived here by her grace. And permit me to add …' He paused, as if unsure of his rights or obligation to speak his mind. 'There is little doubt that Mrs Harcourt's death was facilitated by a blatant disregard for her health.'

'What are you saying?' Julia Harcourt screamed.

'I'm saying that, while there is no substantive proof that you and your husband nearly starved the woman to death – not to mention leaving her in a state of filth that your servants were too afraid to manage, for fear of being put out on the streets – I would not hesitate for one moment to notify the police and demand a formal investigation. They might find no proof, but the scandal of that investigation would ruin you socially. So yes, while your husband is her rightful heir, it was very much within her legal rights to bequeath her property and possessions as she saw fit. Therefore, this house is now the property of her heirs, the staff as constituted. If you contest that, you will lose the cottage in Hertfordshire. It will be sold, and the proceeds added to the estate. Is that what you wish? It can certainly be accomplished, and I will see to it.'

Julia Harcourt drew in breath and let it out soundlessly.

Her husband intervened. 'No, Mr O'Mara, that is not what I wish. I am ashamed to say, there is some justice in it.'

'How dare you?' his wife blurted out, her voice seething with resentment.

He continued as if she had not spoken. He was still looking at Denning 'We would be obliged if we may remain here until the day after Christmas.'

O'Mara looked around the circle of stunned faces. 'Is that the wish of you all?' he asked quietly.

One by one they nodded their agreement. All except Gracie.

'Mrs …?' O'Mara hesitated.

'Mrs Tellman, sir. I'll be going home to my husband and children tonight. I'll miss everyone, but I said I'd be home for Christmas, and I will be.'

She turned to Allsop. 'If I could take the scarf for Charlie?'

O'Mara smiled at Gracie. 'She did not know you when she wrote the will, of course, but she was quite clear in the addition to it. Hearing of your family gave her great pleasure, and she added you to the will with full intent. Now, perhaps you had better pack your cases, and if you wish, I have a carriage outside and would be happy to take you back to your own family.'

'Now?' Gracie was breathless.

'Yes,' said the lawyer. 'I have certain business with Mr Denning to conduct. He will need a great deal of information, and possibly advice, even in the short run, never mind over a period of time into the future.' He turned to Allsop. 'And you are Miss Allsop? Yes, I thought so. If you do decide to start a dressmaking business of your own, you will wish to remain living here, but you will need some practical advice regarding how to begin. The firm will be happy to represent you, unless you already have legal representation of your own?'

For the first time, Allsop was emotionally over-whelmed. 'Thank you, I would be very grateful for that.'

Walters stood up. 'Gracie, may I help you carry your bags? You don't want to be late for your family. It's getting dark already.'

'Yes,' Gracie gulped. 'Yes … sir.' She was not ready. Of course, she was packed and had left the room tidy, empty and very clean. But emotionally … she was not ready. She had been here only a few days, but she had learned to care about these people. They had faced all sorts of deep emotions together, many of them unspoken, but understood nonetheless.

She stood up, and looked once around the room. This might be the last time she saw them. They would be listening in private to O'Mara's advice. What should she say? Goodbye? But that was not enough. Thank you? That seemed out of place. They had done this together, because they cared, and it was right.

Archie sniffed hard. He was looking directly at Gracie. 'I'm gonna learn to read,' he said solemnly. 'All the books in the library.'

'Of course you are,' she agreed. 'And lots of other things as well.'

The tears started down his cheeks, but he smiled.

Gracie swallowed hard. 'Happy Christmas,' she said, then went out through the door.

It did not take long, with Walters' help, to put her few possessions into O'Mara's carriage. Plus, of course, the two scarves and the envelope with the money for the boys.

O'Mara got into the carriage and sat beside her. He was smiling as if he could not help it, nor did he wish to. He asked her for instructions, then passed them on to the driver. He leaned back and gave a sigh of pleasure. 'I have been waiting to read that will for months. I'm sorry to see the old lady go, but she was more than ready. I like to think her ghost was watching us, not with spite for her family, but perhaps a shred of satisfaction. She paid back the kindness of all those who risked their jobs to afford her the little comfort that they could.'

'Can you take Millie back?' she asked. 'For Christmas?'

'Of course.' He was still smiling. 'I'd like to see how they are this evening.'

'Will you go on helping them? They're not used to being in control.' There was so much more that she wanted to say, but it seemed in some ways to imply they were not competent.

'Don't worry,' O'Mara said with amusement at her difficulty. 'The old lady thought of that. It's part of my duty that I have been instructed in and paid for, that I should oversee all the actions that might prove any problem. They will make a few mistakes – everybody does – but not serious ones. Don't worry,' he repeated, and then settled even more comfortably into his seat and gave a sigh of satisfaction. 'Have a happy Christmas.'

They remained in that comfortable silence until they reached Gracie's house and pulled up at the kerb. It was already dark. The front door opened, letting out a shaft of golden light. Charlie stood in the middle of it, peering at the carriage.

Gracie climbed out.

'Mam!' Charlie shouted joyfully. 'Mam! I knew you'd come!' She left the door wide open and ran towards the carriage, where Gracie was climbing out. She ran straight into Gracie's arms, clinging on to her like a limpet.

Then Tommy and Vic came out and ran into her arms as well. Tellman appeared in the doorway, smiling. Gracie looked up. 'Tell Millie to get her things. Mr O'Mara will take her back home. He'll tell her what happened, and all the good things that will happen from now on.'

A few minutes later, Millie hugged them all goodbye and went off with O'Mara in the carriage.

It was very late. Gracie was seated on the floor at her husband's feet, leaning against him and basking in the warmth of the fire. Tommy and Vic were asleep on the sofa, with Vic's head in his father's lap, and Tommy nestled beside him. Charlie was wrapped up in her bright crimson scarf, upright against the pillows on the second armchair, sound asleep.

Outside, the wind rose a little, pattering rain on the window.

Softly, in the distance, came the sound of Christmas bells.

We hope you have enjoyed reading Anne Perry's enthralling festive mystery.

Don't miss her other Christmas novellas, as well as her many bestselling crime novels . . .

DISCOVER FESTIVE MYSTERIES

FROM THE INIMITABLE

ANNE PERRY

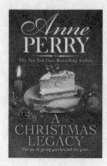  

DON'T MISS ANNE PERRY'S LATEST THRILLERS
OF ESPIONAGE AND MURDER SET BETWEEN
THE WORLD WARS,
THE ELENA STANDISH SERIES

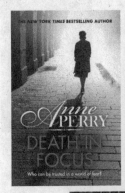

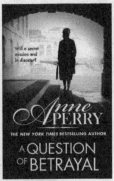

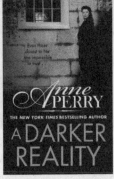

AND A NEW GENERATION OF PITT NOVELS,
FEATURING THOMAS'S BARRISTER SON, DANIEL,
IN THE DANIEL PITT SERIES

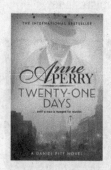
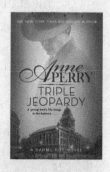

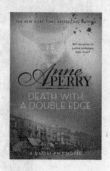

GO TO WWW.ANNEPERRY.CO.UK
TO FIND OUT MORE

FOR MORE FROM ANNE PERRY, TRY
THE THOMAS PITT SERIES

---

BETHLEHEM ROAD
HIGHGATE RISE
BELGRAVE SQUARE
FARRIERS' LANE
THE HYDE PARK HEADSMAN
TRAITORS GATE
PENTECOST ALLEY
ASHWORTH HALL
BRUNSWICK GARDENS
BEDFORD SQUARE
HALF MOON STREET
THE WHITECHAPEL CONSPIRACY
SOUTHAMPTON ROW
SEVEN DIALS
LONG SPOON LANE
BUCKINGHAM PALACE GARDENS
BETRAYAL AT LISSON GROVE
DORCHESTER TERRACE
MIDNIGHT AT MARBLE ARCH
DEATH ON BLACKHEATH
THE ANGEL COURT AFFAIR
TREACHERY AT LANCASTER GATE
MURDER ON THE SERPENTINE

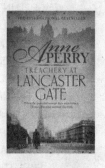

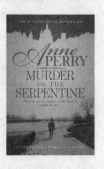

---

GO TO WWW.ANNEPERRY.CO.UK
TO FIND OUT MORE

# DISCOVER THE
# WILLIAM MONK SERIES

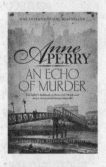

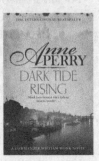

GO TO WWW.ANNEPERRY.CO.UK
TO FIND OUT MORE